"You'd better get out of that dress."

He couldn't mean...? Was her mother right? Did all men just want to...?

Rachel wrapped an arm around the thick wooden bedpost, half clinging to it, half shrinking behind it. Her mouth was dry, her stomach quivering with fear. Shaking violently, she turned, offering her back to him and bending her head forward so he could reach the top of the zip. It seemed to take an eternity. At last his long fingers brushed the hair off the nape of her neck and skimmed over the sensitized skin of her shoulders, leaving a shivering trail of sensation in their wake.

She'd thought she was afraid of his touch, but this was something quite different. Something she'd thought she was incapable of experiencing, which had been unfurling inside her since he'd first held her against him.

With a thud of shock and a rush of liquid heat, she realized the sensation that was quickening her pulse and filling her limbs with honeyed warmth was not fear.

It was arousal.

A self-confessed romance junkie, **INDIA GREY** was just thirteen years old when she first sent off for the Mills & Boon writers' guidelines. She can still recall the thrill of getting the large brown envelope, with its distinctive logo, through the letterbox, and subsequently whiled away many a dull school day staring out of the window and dreaming of the perfect hero. She kept those guidelines with her for the next ten years, tucking them carefully inside the cover of each new diary in January, and beginning every list of New Year's resolutions with the words *Start novel*. In the meantime she gained a degree in English literature from Manchester University and, in a stroke of genius on the part of the gods of romance, met her gorgeous future husband on the very last night of their three years there. The last fifteen years have been spent blissfully buried in domesticity, and heaps of pink washing generated by three small daughters, but she has never really stopped daydreaming about romance. She's just profoundly grateful to have finally got an excuse to do it legitimately!

MISTRESS: HIRED FOR THE BILLIONAIRE'S PLEASURE
INDIA GREY

~ HIRED: FOR THE BOSS'S PLEASURE ~

HARLEQUIN®

TORONTO • NEW YORK • LONDON
AMSTERDAM • PARIS • SYDNEY • HAMBURG
STOCKHOLM • ATHENS • TOKYO • MILAN • MADRID
PRAGUE • WARSAW • BUDAPEST • AUCKLAND

Recycling programs
for this product may
not exist in your area.

ISBN-13: 978-0-373-52705-2
ISBN-10:   0-373-52705-5

MISTRESS: HIRED FOR THE BILLIONAIRE'S PLEASURE

First North American Publication 2009.

www.eHarlequin.com

Printed in U.S.A.

MISTRESS: HIRED FOR THE BILLIONAIRE'S PLEASURE

For all the heroes of the RAF...
and for one in particular.
F.W.—with thanks.

PROLOGUE

'It's not good news, I'm afraid.'

Orlando Winterton didn't flinch. A thousand years of aristocratic breeding and a lifetime of ruthless self-control made his lean, dark face perfectly expressionless as the ophthalmic consultant looked down at the file on the mirror-shiny expanse of Victorian mahogany that separated them.

'The test results show that your field of vision is significantly impaired in the central section, indicating that the cells of the macula may be prematurely breaking down...'

'Spare me the science, Andrew.' Orlando's voice was harsh. 'Let's just cut straight to the bit where you tell me what you can do about it.'

There was a small pause. Orlando felt his hands tighten on the arms of the discreetly expensive leather chair as he tried to read the expression on Andrew Parkes's clever, careful face. But the blurring in the centre of his vision that had brought him here was already advanced enough to make this kind of sensitive judgement difficult. He waited, listening for clues in the other man's tone.

'Ah. Well, I'm afraid the answer to that is not very much.'

Orlando said nothing, but he felt his head jerk back slightly, as if he had been struck. There it was, that soft note of pity he had dreaded. A quiet death knell.

'I'm sorry, Orlando.'

'Don't be. Just tell me what's going to happen. Will I still be able to fly?'

Andrew Parkes sighed. It was never easy being the bearer of news like this, but in Orlando Winterton's case it was particularly cruel. Andrew had been a friend of Orlando's father, Lord Ashbroke, until his death four years ago, and understood that in joining the RAF both of Ashbroke's sons were following a long and distinguished family tradition. He also knew of the intense rivalry that burned between Orlando and his younger brother Felix. Both were exceptional pilots, both had risen through the ranks with astonishing speed to hold one of the most envied roles in the Royal Air Force—that of flight commander on the cutting-edge, controversial Typhoon Squadron. Orlando, the elder, had recently surpassed Felix by achieving the status of Officer Commanding Weapons Flight—the highest flying position.

To cut short such a glittering career was a terrible blow to have to deal. There was no pleasant way of doing it, so he was left only with the option of being honest.

'No. Given the information I have in front of me I have no choice but to sign you off with immediate effect. It'll take a while for a firm diagnosis to be made, but at the moment all the signs point to a condition called Stargardt's Macular Dystrophy.'

Still Orlando didn't move. Only the muscle flickering beneath the lean, tanned plane of his cheek hinted at the emotion that must be raging beneath his impassive exterior.

'I can still see. I can still fly. Surely this can remain confidential?'

The consultant shook his head. 'Not as far as the RAF are concerned. Who you choose to tell in your personal life is your decision. Your ability to live a completely normal life will be unaffected, for the moment at least, so no one will need to know until you feel able to tell them.'

'I see.' Orlando gave a short, bitter laugh which was edged with despair. 'My life will be normal "for the moment at least." I guess you're about to tell me all that's going to change?'

'I'm afraid it's a degenerative condition.'

Orlando stood up abruptly. 'Thanks for your time, Andrew.'

'Orlando, wait—please—there must be questions you need to ask…other things you want to know…?'

His voice trailed off as Orlando turned back to face him. His height and the powerful breadth of his shoulders made the desolation on his face all the more terrible.

'No. You've told me all I need to hear.'

'I have some literature for you to read when you're ready.' Andrew slid a leaflet across the desk and continued in a tone of forced optimism. 'A diagnosis like this can take some time to sink in, and it helps if you have someone to talk to. Are you still seeing that super girl? Quite a high-flyer—lawyer, wasn't she?'

Orlando paused, seeming to weigh up his answer. 'Arabella. She's a corporate financier. Yes, we're still…seeing each other.'

'Good.' Andrew gave a relieved smile, and added carefully, 'And Felix? He's home at the moment, isn't he?'

'Yes. We were both taking some time out at Easton before beginning another tour of duty next week.' He smiled bleakly. 'It looks like he'll be going alone.'

Emerging from the consulting room into the London street, Orlando blinked.

It was an overcast January day, but even the cold grey light filtering through the dark clouds hurt his eyes. He didn't let himself hesitate, refused to reach out for the reassurance of the handrail at the side of the stone steps.

He would do this without support of any kind. From anyone.

There was a hiss of air brakes and a bus moved away from the kerb in front of him, just as a shaft of thin sunlight broke through the cloud. Right ahead, high up on the building opposite, was an advertising hoarding, displaying a huge poster for some classical music CD. It showed a red-haired girl in a billowing ivy-green evening dress.

It was a picture he'd noticed countless times around London

since he'd been on leave, but he was suddenly struck by the realisation that until now he'd never really *seen* it. Like so much else. Letting out a deep, shuddering breath, he tipped his head back and gazed up at her. Her huge, luminous amber-coloured eyes seemed to be full of sadness as they locked with his, and though her pale pink lips were curved into the ghost of a smile they seemed to tremble with uncertainty.

At that moment it hit him.

Gazing up at her, he saw with brutal clarity everything he was losing. And he felt the darkness that would soon engulf his vision wrap itself around his heart.

CHAPTER ONE

One year later

IT WAS barely light as Rachel let herself out of the front door of The Old Rectory and closed it silently behind her. The damp chill of early morning curled itself around her, and her slow outdrawn breath made misty plumes in the bitter February air.

Already the house was stirring, but only with the impersonal band of cleaners and caterers who had come in early to obliterate the traces of last night's party and prepare for today's celebrations. Even so, making her way carefully across the grass, Rachel felt the back of her neck prickle with fear that she was being watched. Swiftly she headed in the direction of the high hedge that separated the old house from the churchyard, not really knowing why—only that she had to escape from the house and try to find somewhere where she could think.

And breathe. And step outside of the relentless march of events towards the moment she couldn't even bear to contemplate.

In her hand she carried a half empty bottle of champagne that she had picked up from the table in the hall on the way out. Last night's pre-wedding party, for a handful of the most influential of Carlos's music industry friends, had apparently gone on into the small hours—although she herself had gone to bed around midnight. No doubt he'd be furious with her for not staying and 'making an impression', or chatting up the right people, but her head had ached and her heart had been leaden with dread at the coming day. She'd pleaded tiredness, but had ended up lying awake until the last cars had left in a noisy series of slamming doors and shouted farewells at about three a.m., bearing Carlos off to the plush country house hotel where he was to spend the final night of his long years of bachelor freedom.

And in the darkness Rachel had wrapped her arms around herself and shivered with horror at the thought of what the following night would bring.

Ducking though a low archway cut into the beech hedge, she found herself in the churchyard. A thin mist hung low over the ground, giving the place an eerie air of melancholy which suited her mood perfectly. Tugging the sleeves of her thick cashmere sweater down over her hands, she hugged the bottle to her and walked slowly around to the other side of the church, out of sight of the house. Everything was grey, black, silver in the early morning light. She tipped her face up to the leaden sky, watching the rooks circling above the spire of the church, and felt nothing but despair.

A gust of icy wind whipped her hair over her face and made her shiver. Up ahead, in the shadow of an ancient yew tree, stood the largest grave of all, set slightly apart from the rest, topped by an imposing stone angel with its carved wings partly furled and its pale face downturned. Rachel found herself drawn towards it.

Beneath the canopy of the yew it was sheltered from the wind. The angel gazed down at her with blank eyes, and the expression on its sculpted face was one of infinite compassion and resignation.

He's seen it all before, she thought bleakly. Those pale, sightless eyes must have witnessed countless weddings and funerals, extremes of joy and tragedy. She wondered whether there had ever been another bride who would rather be going to her own funeral than her wedding.

Sinking down onto the dry earth beneath the angel's cold, pale feet, she took a swig of champagne, then leaned her cheek against the lichened stone. The sides of the tomb were carved with rows of names and dates, some of which were worn away almost to illegibility and obscured by moss. But the name nearest to her was still sharp and clear. Tracing her fingers over it, she read the words.

The Hon. Felix Alexander Winterton
of Easton Hall
Killed in active service to his country
HE GAVE HIS TODAY THAT WE MIGHT HAVE
OUR TOMORROW

She looked up at the angel with a watery smile and raised the champagne bottle. 'Cheers, Felix,' she whispered. 'But in my case that was a real wasted gesture.'

Orlando hardly noticed the cold as he got out of the car and walked towards the churchyard. Cold seemed to be his natural element these days. Cold, and gathering darkness, of course.

His last visit to Andrew Parkes had not brought any positive news. His sight was deteriorating more rapidly than Parkes had initially predicted, and he'd advised Orlando that it was now imperative he gave up driving.

He would. Today was the last time. The anniversary of Felix's death. He'd come down to his grave early enough to avoid any traffic, taking the private lanes through the estate. At high speed.

The nature of the condition was that his peripheral vision was pretty much unaffected, while his central field of vision was nothing more than a blur—like a dark fingerprint on a camera lens. Getting around wasn't yet a problem, but it was the finer details that were quickly slipping away from him. He could no longer read faces, recognise people without them announcing themselves, or carry out easily the million small things he had once done without even thinking. Fastening the buttons on a shirt. Making coffee. Reading his mail.

But he would die before he let other people see that. Which was why he had come back to Easton, and solitude.

Pausing in the shelter of the lychgate, he looked up to where a group of rooks circled above the church, their ragged wings black against a grey sky. Everything was fading to the same monochrome, he thought bleakly, screwing up his eyes to scan the churchyard, where the headstones looked bone white against the dark fringe of bare trees and the shadowy bulk of the yew over the Winterton plot.

Something caught the corner of his eye. A flash of red in the gloom. He tilted his head, standing very still as he tried to work out what it was.

A fox? Slinking back to its earth after a night out hunting?

And then he located it again,

A girl. A red-headed girl was sitting on Felix's grave.

'What the hell do you think you're doing?'

Rachel's head snapped upwards. A man stood in front of her, towering over her, his long dark coat and dishevelled black hair making him look both beautiful and menacing. His face was every bit as hard and cold as that of the stone angel, but without any trace of compassion.

'I—nothing! I was just…'

She struggled to stand up, but her legs were cramped from sitting on the ground, her feet numb with cold. Instantly she felt his hands close around her arms as he pulled her to her feet. For a moment she was crushed against him, and she felt the wonderful warmth and strength that radiated from his body before he thrust her away. Still keeping his vice-like grip on her upper arm with one hand, he removed the champagne bottle with the other, swilling the contents around as if gauging how much was left.

'I think that explains it.' His lip curled in distaste. 'Isn't it a little early? Or do you have something particularly pressing to celebrate?'

'No.' She gave a short laugh, and had to clap her hand to her mouth as it threatened to turn into a sob. 'I have absolutely nothing at all to celebrate. I was aiming more for Dutch courage.

Or oblivion.' She could feel embarrassing tears begin to slide down her cold cheeks and gave an apologetic smile, stroking a hand over the weathered stone. 'Peaceful oblivion. With lovely, heroic Felix here.'

The dark man didn't return the smile, letting go of her so abruptly that she stumbled backwards and had to lean on the gravestone for support.

'He'll be thrilled to know that a little thing like death hasn't made him lose his touch with women.'

The bitterness etched into the lean planes of his face made Rachel wince. She took in the dark shadows under his slanting eyes, the crease of anguish between his highly arched black brows. Horrified realisation dawned.

'Oh, God, I'm so sorry…you knew him?'

There was a pause. And then he held out his hand with a bleak smile that briefly illuminated the stark beauty of his face.

'Orlando Winterton. Felix's brother.'

She took his hand and, registering the warmth and steadiness of his grip, felt a sudden irrational urge to hold on for dear life. For a brief moment his fingers closed around hers, strong and steady, and she found herself wishing he would never let go.

He withdrew his hand, and she felt the colour surge into her cheeks.

'I'm Rachel. And I'm sorry…about your brother. Was he a soldier?'

'Pilot. RAF. Shot down in the Middle East,' Orlando said tersely.

'How terrible,' she said quietly, curling up her fingers. They tingled where his skin had warmed them.

He shrugged. 'It happens. It's all part of the job.'

'You're a pilot too?'

'Was.'

'It must take incredible courage. To know that every day when you go to work you're staring death in the face.'

He let out a harsh laugh. 'I think there are worse things to stare at than death.'

Rachel sighed, sinking down onto the dry earth at the foot of the tomb again. 'Tell me about it.'

Above her, Orlando Winterton and Felix's angel towered like twin protectors. She leaned her head back against the stone and lifted the bottle towards them before taking a long swig. 'To courage—the real kind. And to Dutch courage—which isn't nearly so honourable, but sometimes has to suffice.'

From the edge of his vision Orlando had an impression of dark eyes in a pale face, a generous trembling mouth, a glorious tumble of fiery hair that stirred a memory in the back of his mind and left him with a sudden fierce longing to see her properly. He could sense the despair rising from her like a scent, but whether this was due to the peculiar instinct that had developed as his sight deserted him or because the feeling was so bloody familiar he couldn't be sure.

She held out the bottle to him. He took it, but didn't drink, instead setting it down on top of the Winterton tomb. 'So, Rachel, what's so bad that you're reduced to sitting out here in the freezing cold drinking with the dead?'

She gave a mirthless laugh. 'You do *not* want to know.'

She was right. He didn't. His own suffering was enough to occupy him on a full-time basis. So why did he find himself saying, 'I usually decide for myself what I want and what I don't want.'

Rachel looked up at him. He was staring straight ahead, and there was something in the dark stillness of his face that made her want very much to confide in him.

'I'm getting married,' she said desolately. 'Today.'

She saw one dark brow shoot up before his face regained its habitual blankness. 'Is that all? Congratulations.'

'Uh-uh. It's not a "congratulations" situation. It's…'

Her voice trailed off as she tried to convey the awfulness of what lay ahead. This afternoon, standing in church before people she mostly neither knew nor cared about making vows she didn't mean… And worse, much worse, knowing that tonight she and Carlos would be man and wife, with all the expectations that carried.

Orlando Winterton shrugged his broad, dark shoulders, his gaze fixed straight ahead. He looked so distant, so controlled, so very, very strong that she felt her chest lurch. How could he understand? She couldn't imagine that this man had ever bowed to the will of anyone else in his life.

'Weddings don't generally happen by accident or without warning. Presumably you had some say in it?' He levered himself up from the gravestone and, thrusting his hands deep into the pockets of his coat, began to move away.

'No,' she said in a low voice.

There was something in the way that she said it that made Orlando stop, turn, and walk back towards her. His deep-set slanting eyes were the most extraordinary clear green, she noticed, and he had a strange, intense way of looking at her, his head tilted backwards slightly in an attitude of distant hauteur.

'You're being forced into this?'

Rachel sighed heavily. 'Well, there's no gun against my head… But, yes. Forced pretty much covers it.'

The last thing he wanted to do was get involved, but his sense of duty, dormant for a year beneath self-pity and bitterness, had seemingly chosen this moment to rouse itself. Wearily he rubbed a hand over his eyes. 'In what way?'

'There's no way out,' she said slowly. 'No Plan B. No choice. This wedding is the culmination of a lifetime of work by my mother.' She laughed. 'If I don't go through with it she'll probably kill me.'

But that was almost preferable to what Carlos would do to her if she stayed and married him. She knew, because he'd done it to her already.

'You can't get married to please your mother.'

The words were laced with scorn, and Rachel felt her head snap back as if she'd just had an ice cube dropped down her spine.

'You don't know my mother. She's…'

She hesitated, shaking her head, trying to find a word for Elizabeth Campion's single-minded obsession with her daughter's musical career; the combination of guile and icy manipulation that would have made Machiavelli green with envy, which had enabled her to bring about the ultimate coup in the form of Rachel's engagement to Carlos Vincente, one of the industry's most influential conductors.

'What? A convicted killer?' Orlando's voice was hard and mocking. 'A cold-blooded psychopath? Head of a crack team of hired assassins?'

His cruelty made her gasp. 'No, of course not. But—' It was impossible to keep the desperation out of her voice. She so badly wanted to make him see what she was up against, but the words darted around in her head, refusing to be pinned down, while all the time he held her in that cool, detached gaze. 'Oh, what's the point? Just forget it. I can't make you understand, so there's no point in trying. Please, just leave me alone!'

'To drink yourself into a stupor? If that's what you want…'

He turned away, and Rachel felt a surge of panic. She had to grip the stony folds of the angel's robes to stop herself from reaching out to hold him back. It was ridiculous, of course; he was nothing more than a passing stranger. But something about the intensity in his face, the bleak self-control in his voice, the immense strength in his shoulders, had made her believe for a moment that he could help her.

Rescue her.

'It's not what I want, but I have no choice!'

He stopped and slowly faced her again. He seemed to look right past her face and into her soul.

'Of course you do. You're young. You're *alive*,' he said with ironic emphasis, gesturing with one elegant hand towards his brother's grave. 'I'd say you have a choice. What you really lack, Rachel, is courage.'

Rachel felt her mouth open in shock and outrage as she watched him walk away. He moved slowly, almost wearily, in spite of his endlessly long legs and athletic build.

He knew nothing—*nothing* about her. How dared he say she lacked courage?

He was way off the mark. Wasn't he?

Courage. Mentally she examined the word. It wasn't a quality she'd ever been taught to value or develop. Obedience, yes. Discipline, perseverance, patience, selflessness—yes, yes, yes, yes…

Not courage. Courage had always seemed like just another word for selfishness.

Orlando Winterton disappeared from view through the gate to the road, and a moment later she heard the roar of a car engine starting up. Straining forwards, she saw a low dark sports car speed past in a shower of gravel and take the unmarked turning to the left of the churchyard. In the silence following its disappearance she was suddenly aware that she was gripping the carved robes of the angel so hard her short fingernails ached.

She felt bereft.

Closing her eyes, she allowed herself to remember the feeling of his hands on her arms, and the moment when she had been held against his chest. She felt again the roughness of his thick woollen sweater against her cheek, smelled the warm, faint tang of expensive aftershave that had clung to the collar of his long, exquisitely tailored black coat.

In that moment she'd felt as if she was safe. As if she'd come home. As if she'd finally found the shadowy figure she'd spent her childhood yearning for—the one man who would protect her from—

'Rachel!'

Her eyes flew open as she recognised her mother's voice, and without thinking she darted back into the cover of the yew tree, hiding behind the vast slab of stone beside her. For a moment all was silent as she crouched there, her heart pounding inside her chest, her cheek resting against the chilly stone where Felix Winterton's name was carved.

'Rachel!'

The voice was closer now, and Rachel knew only too well

its shrill note of exasperation. *I'm twenty-three years old and here I am, hiding from my mother like a naughty child*. She squeezed her eyes shut and suddenly the face of Orlando Winterton swam into focus in the darkness, with that hard, bleak smile of his.

What you really lack is courage.

She hesitated, then stood up slowly.

Dressed in a figure-hugging pink velour tracksuit and last night's high-heeled mules, Elizabeth Campion was making her way in Rachel's direction with unerring accuracy, and the expression on her well-maintained face was murderous.

'I'm here.'

For a wonderful moment Elizabeth was lost for words as she watched her daughter emerge from the shadow of the monument, then the full force of her fury was unleashed.

'What in heaven's name are you doing?'

Rachel steeled herself against Elizabeth's indignant screech, letting her mind return to the last person who had asked her that. Except that Orlando Winterton hadn't said 'heaven'. She pictured his dark, tormented expression, concentrated on reproducing in her mind the exact gritty rasp of his voice as he had said 'hell'.

'Well? I'm waiting!'

With huge effort Rachel dragged herself back to her mother. 'I went for a walk.'

'You *went for a walk*?' repeated Elizabeth, like an apoplectic parrot. 'Saints preserve us! *Why* do you have to be so selfish, Rachel? Today of all days? Haven't I got enough to do with all the wedding arrangements, without having to chase around after you as well because you're just too selfish and immature to get yourself organised? Hmm?'

Reaching the path, Rachel opened her mouth to reply, but her mother had only paused for breath and wasn't actually expecting an answer.

'Carlos phoned. I had to tell him you were in the bath. Lord only knows what he'd say if he knew that you'd *gone for a walk.*' She made it sound as if Rachel had been skateboarding down the motorway.

'I thought it was bad luck for the groom to speak to the bride before the wedding?' said Rachel sarcastically. 'I'd hate anything to spoil our chances of a wonderful happy-ever-after.'

Her mother threw her a venomous glance. 'Don't you dare start all that now, young lady,' she hissed. 'You'll do well to remember how lucky you are to be marrying Carlos.'

Rachel stopped and swung round to face her mother. 'Rubbish! He couldn't give a damn about me! He doesn't love—'

'Shut up! Just *shut up!*' Elizabeth's face was contorted with rage. 'You think you're so clever, don't you? Well, let me tell you something, Rachel. *Love* is nothing but a silly fantasy. It means nothing. *Nothing!* Your father told me he loved me, and where did that get me? I nearly died giving him a baby he didn't even stay around to watch grow up. *Love* doesn't bring you *security*.'

Rachel felt a jolt as the word lodged in her brain like a bullet hitting the bullseye. For a moment she felt dazed and disorientated as conflicting images and sensations raced through her head. Orlando's hands on her arms, holding her up. Carlos's fingers digging into her thighs, hard and insistent, on that awful night in Vienna when he—

She had survived by ruthlessly separating herself from the person who had endured all that. That was Rachel Campion, disciplined pianist, obedient fiancée, dutiful daughter. Not the real her. But the trouble was it was getting increasingly difficult to remember who the real Rachel was.

She'd caught a glimpse of her back there in the graveyard. She was someone who wanted to be courageous. And secure.

She went back into the house and closed the door very quietly behind her.

CHAPTER TWO

As HE passed the gatehouse into the long straight drive up to Easton Hall, Orlando put his foot down and felt the world fall away in a dizzying rush. The frustration and fury that had needled him on the short drive home was temporarily anaesthetised in the blissful blur of speed.

This was the place where he and Felix had raced—first on their bikes as small boys, then later on horseback and motorbikes. It was here that, returning home for his twenty-first, Felix's brand-new Alpha Romeo had been written off as Orlando had overtaken him and forced him into the moat.

Their rivalry had been as strong as their love for each other.

Protected by birth and privilege, made arrogant by wealth and good looks, they had thought they were invincible. But all it had meant in the end was that they'd had further to fall. All the money in the world, an unblemished bloodline and the looks of an angel hadn't protected Felix from a rocket attack in his Typhoon, and the lottery of genes that had made up Orlando's perfect face was now destroying his sight.

There was a certain biblical morality to it.

All too soon Orlando reached the bridge across the old moat and had to slow down. The drive narrowed as it passed through the high gateposts to Easton Hall, and he drove more carefully round the house to the garages at the back. Bringing the car to a standstill in the brick-paved courtyard that had once housed grand carriages, he let his head fall forward to rest on the steering wheel. His hands still held it, as if he couldn't bear to let go, to take the keys out of the ignition for the last time.

He was giving up his independence.

He felt his mouth jerk into an ironic smile as he thought of the girl in the graveyard. He'd been harsh with her, but her helpless distress had been like acid in his own open wounds. *She* could take control of her situation. For him, control was inexorably slipping from him, with the inevitability of day sliding into night; there was nothing, *nothing* he could do. And this was the first measure of his failure. Slowly he opened the door and got stiffly out, blinking in the thin grey light.

'Will you be needing the car again today, sir?'

Orlando hadn't seen the man emerge from the doorway of one of the outbuildings, but he recognised his voice easily enough. George had worked for Lord Ashbroke since Orlando and Felix were children.

'No.' *Not today. Not ever.*

Soon, Orlando supposed, he would have to tell George. Ask him to take on the duties of a chauffeur.

'Shall I put her away for you?'

'Thanks.' Orlando took the keys from the ignition and let his fingers close around them tightly for a moment. Then he tossed them in George's direction and walked across the yard into the house.

'There. You look lovely, darling.' Elizabeth Campion's hands fluttered around Rachel's face like tiny birds, smoothing a wayward curl here, teasing a fold of frothy lace there. The church bells seemed horribly loud, pealing out their tumbling scales with a threatening leer, but at least it made conversation unnecessary.

Beneath the shroud of her veil Rachel stood impassive.

She was glad of the veil. It separated her from the rest of the world in a way that seemed particularly appropriate, filtering out the unwelcome ministrations of her mother, screening her own increasingly desperate thoughts and emotions from view. In the mirror her reflection was smooth and expressionless, with its pure, blanked-out face.

'Right, then. I'd better go over to church,' Elizabeth said brightly, as she checked her watch and gave Rachel's dress a last little tweak. Chosen by Carlos, it was cut in the Empire style of a regency heroine—which, Carlos had said, would charm the Americans when she sat at the piano later. Elizabeth handed her a bouquet of waxy white flowers. 'Here, don't forget these. Now, wait until the verger comes across to get you. And then it's your big moment! For God's sake see if you can manage a smile, darling, please…'

The shrouded figure in the mirror nodded almost imperceptibly. Elizabeth bustled around, adjusting her large peacock-blue hat, spritzing on another cloud of perfume, picking up a pair of black gloves and thrusting her hands into them like a surgeon preparing to cut, before finally reaching the door.

She stopped, and Rachel felt herself go very still, waiting for a sign or a word that would mean all this could be stopped. Elizabeth's face was thoughtful.

'Such a shame your father didn't have the decency to stay around for this. It's the one day of his life when he could have made himself useful. Oh, well, darling. The verger's a very nice man. He'll be about ten minutes, I should think.'

Then she was gone.

A gust of air from the door rippled Rachel's veil.

Beneath it, Rachel felt as if she was choking. Fury and despair swelled inside her, and without thinking what she was doing she found herself tearing off the veil as a series of shuddering sobs ripped through her.

She had to get away.

Glancing wildly around her, she picked up the keys to the car Carlos had bought her as an engagement present. She had always felt the gesture had been akin to putting a caged bird beside an open window, but suddenly it was as if the door to her cage had been left open and she had one fleeting chance to fly.

She ran down the stairs, her wedding shoes clattering on the polished wood, her breath coming in shaky gasps. Fumbling with the catch on the front door, she peered out for a second, before throwing it open and rushing across the gravel to the car.

Her hands were shaking so much she could hardly turn the key in the ignition, and then, when she did manage to start the engine, she shot forward with a sickeningly loud shower of gravel. She didn't dare look up at the house as she accelerated out of the drive and onto the road, wincing as she made the tyres squeal on the tarmac in her panic to get away. Whimpering quietly, she cast an anxious glance in the mirror, half expecting to see Carlos run out onto the drive of The Old Rectory, or her mother appear at the roadside, a bright flash of peacock-blue in the February gloom.

The main entrance to the church where all the guests had gathered was around the other side, but still the road seemed horribly exposed, and almost without thinking she found herself taking the narrow turning alongside the church, down which she'd watched Orlando Winterton drive that morning.

It was a single-track road, overhung with high hedges and spiked, naked branches of hawthorn that made it almost like driving through a tunnel. She leaned forward over the steering wheel, gripping it so hard that sharp arrows of pain vibrated along the taut tendons of her hands and down her wrists.

Behind her, the peal of bells echoed eerily through the leaden air, and the sound made her press her foot harder on the accelerator, trying to put as much distance between her and the church as quickly as possible. Ahead of her the lane twisted around blind bends, making it impossible to get any idea of where she was going.

She hadn't even thought of that. Where *was* she going?

In fact, where was she? Panic pumped through her in icy bursts. Looking around her wildly, she wondered whether anyone had realised she was gone yet. Would the verger have found her missing by now? Maybe it wasn't too late to go back. No one would have to know. All she had to do was find somewhere to turn round in this godforsaken lane. She could slip in as quietly as she'd left, replace the veil, and let the rest of her life continue as planned.

Carlos and her mother were right. She couldn't possibly cut it on her own. She couldn't even run away without getting lost.

It had started to rain, a thin mist of drops that beaded the windscreen and blurred the world beyond to a watery grey. Frantically trying to remember how to work the windscreen wipers, Rachel eventually located the right lever, only to discover that the blur was caused not by rain but by tears.

The road was bumpy and potholed, and there was nowhere to turn. She pressed her foot harder to the accelerator, trying to make the noise of the engine drown out the sound of the church bells in the distance. They were fainter now, drifting eerily over the dank, drab fields with a ghostly melancholy that was horribly funereal. The hairs rose on the back of her neck. Suddenly everything seemed sinister—loaded with menace. Her heart thudded madly as she glanced again and again in the rearview mirror, expecting to see the headlamps of Carlos's huge black car getting closer, dazzling, hypnotising, until they engulfed her.

Someone must have seen her go. Someone must have heard. He would have guessed that she had gone with that terrifying instinct he had for sensing her fear and exploiting it until she was helpless to do anything but submit to him…

She could almost feel his hot breath on her neck, and, letting out a whimper of terror, had to look quickly over her shoulder to reassure herself she was imagining it.

Twisting her head back again, she saw that the road in front had narrowed suddenly into a low-sided bridge. She swerved, but did so too sharply, cringing at the sickening sound of metal against stone as the nearside wing glanced off the wall. Numb with horror, she kept going, accelerating off the bridge with a screech of tyres and swinging out onto a straight stretch of road. She should stop, check the damage to the car, but darkness crouched menacingly in the hedges and fields beyond, harbouring all manner of nameless horrors—all of which paled into insignificance at the thought of Carlos gaining on her. She imagined him pulling up alongside her as she stood in the deserted, darkling lane, getting out of the car and coming towards her with that look in his eyes that she would never be able to forget…

A sob tore through her, and she felt herself buckle, as if she'd been punched in the stomach, as the memories bubbled up through the thin crust that had sealed them in, like a mental scab. Her lungs screamed for air. It was all she could do to keep her hands on the wheel and not fall into the yawning chasm of panic that had opened up beneath her.

What you lack, Rachel, is courage.

Orlando's voice cut through the fog—calm, steady, reassuringly blank. And then suddenly up ahead she saw the shape of a large building, dark against the pewter sky, and twin gateposts reared up on either side of the road. Weeping with relief, she sped towards them as a dim memory of a story she'd read as a child came back to her—where someone had had to race across a bridge to safety before a headless horseman caught them and all was lost.

She screeched through the gates and slewed the car round on the gravel in front of the huge, dark house, praying there was someone home. Someone who could help her—hide her—in case Carlos was making his way through the dark, dripping lanes towards her.

Turning off the ignition, she sank down in the driver's seat, waiting for her heartbeat to stop reverberating through her entire body and for enough strength to return to her trembling legs to allow her to walk up to that imposing front door. What if there was no answer? She pictured herself knocking, hammering with all her strength as the sound echoed through vast, empty rooms, and all the time the headlights in the distance were growing closer…

And then, as she watched, a soft light spilled out across the gravel as the door opened and a figure appeared. Scrabbling at the door handle with shaking, bloodless fingers, she threw herself out and had to lean against the car for a moment as relief cascaded through her.

A second later relief had turned to anguished recognition.

There in the doorway, like a dark negative image of the angel in the churchyard, stood Orlando Winterton.

Orlando flung open the door and frowned into the gathering darkness. He had heard the sound of tyres skidding on gravel but it took a few seconds for him to bring into focus the very expensive, very damaged silver sports car which looked as if it had been abandoned in front of the house.

Arabella.

She'd phoned last night and announced in that cold, efficient way of hers that she wanted to see him. He couldn't imagine why: everything in Arabella's life was glamorous and high-functioning. She had no room for weakness—a fact which she had made perfectly plain at the time of Orlando's diagnosis. Maybe she'd developed a conscience? he'd thought cynically as he'd slammed the phone down, having told her exactly what she could do.

But she always had liked to have the last word. Orlando's face was like stone as he stood in the doorway, waiting for her to get out of the car. He wondered what tack she would take this time—mockery or seductiveness? Either way, he was immune. That was one thing he could be grateful for: when you lived in hell already, no one could make it any worse.

The car door opened and a slender figure sprang out, ghostly white in the winter gloom. Orlando felt his head jerk upwards slightly as he desperately sought to bring her into his field of vision.

Not Arabella.

She stood against the car, and even with his failing sight, even in the gathering February dusk, he could see that she was trembling. She was wearing a thin white dress that blew against her long legs, and her bright hair was like a beacon in the blurred centre of his vision. It lit up the darkness. Red for danger.

Red for passion.

The girl from the graveyard.

Slowly he walked down the steps towards her. Frozen by the

icy wind that stung her bare arms and whipped her hair across her numb cheeks, Rachel watched him helplessly, suddenly finding that her brain was as frozen as the rest of her, but that something, somewhere deep inside of her just wanted to fling herself into this man's arms.

In the distance she could still hear the discordant peal of the church bells, and she gave her head a little shake, trying to regain a rational hold on the situation. The trouble was, she wasn't sure there was one.

'I'm sorry,' she said, in a voice that was little more than a hoarse croak. 'I didn't mean to come here. I didn't know... The road—I didn't know where it went—I was just...driving...'

He looked down on her from his great height. His massive shoulders were rigid with tension, but his face gave nothing away. 'Driving away from your wedding, I take it?'

'Yes. I couldn't...do it.' She spoke very carefully, breathing slowly and deliberately to keep herself together. 'I waited until the last possible minute to see if something would happen to stop it, but it didn't...and then...I knew I couldn't do it. I ran away... because you were right, I...'

She took another steadying breath, but at that moment the church bells stopped abruptly. Silence seemed to fold around them like fog. Rachel felt her hands fly to her mouth, her eyes widening in horror as the implications of that silence sank in.

They knew. They'd found she was missing. And Carlos... Carlos would be...

Frantically she pushed her fingers through her hair, looking wildly about her as terror gripped her once again. Without knowing what she was doing, she wrenched open the car door.

Orlando was beside her in a flash, his arms closing around her waist, pinning her own arms to her sides and stopping her escape. She struggled against him, twisting her shoulders frantically, but his strength was enormous. Effortlessly he held her against him.

'Let me go! I have to go *now*! They'll come after me and—'

'No!' His voice was like sandpaper. He swung her round to

face him, his hands holding her upper arms again, as they had this morning in the churchyard. 'You're not going anywhere in this state. You're staying here.'

He felt the fight go out of her. She slumped into his hands, so that he was holding her up. Over her head his eyes were fixed on an unseen point in the distance as he gritted his teeth and fought to control the emotions that warred within him—impatience, hostility, exasperation, resentment.

And the prickle of arousal that had fuelled at least some of those.

He felt his mind shut like a steel trap against it. Those feelings had no place in his life now. But it was the scent of her hair that had done it, the weight and warmth of it as she thrashed in his arms that had made him feel momentarily as if he had been punched in the solar plexus.

She raised her head, so he could make out the milk-white curve of her cheek. 'I couldn't stay…' she said dully. 'It's too much to ask…I can't…'

He let her go and took a step away, slamming the car door with unnecessary force. 'Do you have anywhere else to go?'

'No.'

'Well, then,' he said with biting sarcasm, 'let's skip the part where you put up some token resistance, shall we? I think this is one instance where you really don't have a choice, and it's not as if I don't have room.'

Rachel looked up at the house, noticing it properly for the first time. Built of red brick, with a central grey stone porch, its blank windows stretched away from her on both sides, and she could make out a steeply pitched roofline and vast elaborate chimneys against the heavy sky. It was beautiful, but huge and dark and utterly forbidding. Just like its owner.

He had started back towards it, and now looked impatiently over his shoulder.

'What are you waiting for?'

The acid in his tone stung her raw emotions. 'I can't leave the car here…someone might see it… And my things…' she wailed, aware that she sounded like a hysterical child, but too distressed to care.

He stopped and came wearily back towards her, his hand out-stretched. 'Give me the keys and I'll get someone to move the car.'

She handed them to him and watched numbly as he went round to the boot and took out her large designer case.

'You planned your escape well,' he said wryly.

'No…I didn't plan it at all. This was packed yesterday. For tonight…' Her voice trailed off and he gave her a wintry smile.

'Your wedding night. Of course.'

He had to consciously turn his thoughts away from imagining what was in there, selected in anticipation of a very different night from the one that now awaited her. Whatever it was, whatever expensive, seductive confections of silk and lace lay folded carefully inside, she'd have no need of them here. The wing where he intended to put her hadn't been used in a year at least. It was freezing.

It was also as far away from his room as possible.

Following him up a flight of steps and through a hugely high door, Rachel shivered. She felt like Beauty entering the castle of the Beast.

And then she caught sight of her dim reflection in an ornate gilt mirror in the hallway and let out a breath of ironic laughter at the thought.

Beauty? Who was she kidding? Her hair, brushed and tamed by dedicated professionals only a couple of hours ago, had since been swept by both wind and her own frantic fingers, and was now tumbling over her shoulders and around her face, giving her a slightly deranged appearance. Her eyes, expertly made up by a make-up artist, were huge and glittering with unfamiliar shadow in the ashen oval of her face. The dress only added to her appearance of a nineteenth-century waif on her way to the asylum.

Ahead of her, Orlando hesitated in a doorway at the end of the dark hallway, tall, effortlessly elegant, with broad, straight shoulders and that aristocratic upward tilt of his head. She felt a sharp twist somewhere inside her as she glanced up at him.

There was something about him that touched nerves in her that were too sensitive. Too sensual. And that terrified her.

Courage…

'This way.'

The imposing entrance hall opened onto a smaller hallway from which the stairs rose in a graceful sweep around two walls. He had started to ascend, keeping close to the wall and brushing his fingers against the painted panelling as he went. Mesmerised, she watched, feeling her flesh tingle almost as if it could feel that feathery touch. At the top of the stairs he turned to the right, along a dark corridor. Rachel glanced around her, noticing the silk-shaded wall-lights at intervals on the emerald-green walls, wondering why he didn't turn them on. At least the gloom inside allowed her to get a good view of what lay outside, and she paused to look out of one of the windows. It overlooked a courtyard whose walls were formed by the house, built in a square around it. The courtyard was divided into quarters by four dark, square flowerbeds in which nothing grew.

He'd gone ahead, and she had to hurry to catch up, guided only by the echo of his footsteps on the polished oak floorboards. Even in her frozen mental state she was stunned by her surroundings. The house was astonishing.

'In here,' he said curtly, opening a door. Rachel followed him into a large room dominated by a huge marble fireplace and containing little more than a vast canopied bed upon which he threw her case.

'You'd better get out of that dress.'

The dusky afternoon threw deep shadows into the edges of the room. Instantly alarmed and on her guard, she let her gaze fly to his face questioningly. His expression was glacial.

Seemingly oblivious to her distress he strode over to the windows and pulled the curtains shut, plunging the room into velvet blackness.

Inside her chest, her heart hammered a frenzied tattoo.

He couldn't mean…? Was her mother right? Did all men just want to…like Carlos?

She wrapped an arm around a thick wooden bedpost, half clinging to it, half shrinking behind it. Her mouth was dry, her stomach quivering with fear. She felt the air vibrate with his nearness as he passed her in the darkness, heard the soft rustle of his movements, and couldn't quite smother her small whimper.

Then the bedside light clicked on, bathing the room in a welcoming glow and illuminating for a second the hard angles of his face before he moved purposefully towards the door.

'I'll be downstairs.'

She blinked, inhaling sharply in surprise. 'No—Orlando! Wait!'

He stood still. His broad shoulders filled the doorframe as he waited for her to continue, but her throat seemed suddenly to be full of sand. She looked helplessly at him, feeling her mouth open soundlessly for a second before the words came out in a dry croak.

'I…I…need help. With the dress.'

She saw him hesitate, then put a hand up to his head. 'Jeez….' It was something between an exhalation and a curse. And then he was coming back towards her, his face terrifyingly bleak.

Shaking violently, she turned, offering her back to him and bending her head forward so he could reach the top of the zip. She waited, feeling the goosebumps rise on the back of her neck as she anticipated his touch.

It seemed to take an eternity, during which she felt the tension building inside her like water coming to the boil. At last his long fingers brushed the hair off the nape of her neck and skimmed over the sensitised skin of her shoulders, leaving a shivering trail of sensation in their wake. He found the zip, tugged it halfway down, then stepped away, leaving her clinging to the carved bedpost as he wordlessly left the room.

She closed her eyes, desperately wanting to feel some sense of relief, and had to bite her lip against the wave of desolation and longing that washed over her instead.

She'd thought she'd be afraid of his touch, but that was because she was so used to being frightened she almost expected it. But this was something quite different. Something she'd thought she was incapable of experiencing, which had been unfurling inside her since he'd first held her against him in the churchyard.

With a thud of shock and a rush of liquid heat she realised the sensation that was quickening her pulse and filling her limbs with honeyed warmth was not fear.

It was arousal.

CHAPTER THREE

ORLANDO slammed a couple of peppers down onto the marble slab in the kitchen, took a knife from the block, and then reached to switch on the powerful spotlights that were angled down onto the worktop.

The bright light made him flinch.

He frowned, a muscle flickering in his jaw as he balanced the knife in one hand and held a pepper in the other. For a second he hesitated, steadying himself, before he began slicing with swift, savage strokes.

He had made a deliberate decision to accustom himself to the darkness that was fast closing in on him while he still had some sight left. He used artificial light as little as possible, but the kitchen was one place where he could not yet afford to let his fingers take the place of his eyes. His determination to maintain his independence meant that it was vital for him to be able to do as much as possible for himself—without asking for help or admitting weakness. Cooking had been of no interest to him in his old life—Arabella had seen to all of that with flawless competence—but a lot had changed in a year.

Not having to cook was one thing. Not being able to was quite another.

It was easy, he thought brutally, to lock himself up here alone and kid himself that he was doing OK. Managing. So easy to believe he was the person he'd always been when there was no one here to fool.

The arrival of this girl had made him see how mistaken he was.

Upstairs earlier…when she had asked him to unfasten her dress. That was the moment he had been forced to admit that the Orlando Winterton of a year ago was as dead and gone as his brother.

The old Orlando Winterton had been a master in the art of undressing women. The smooth, effortless removal of every kind of feminine garment was something he had excelled at, like everything else. But upstairs just then he had been assailed by panic as his mind had conjured tormenting images of tiny buttons, delicate hooks, and he had opened his mouth to tell her he couldn't possibly do it. The words hadn't come. He'd been afraid to tell her. Unable to deal with sensing her recoil, as Arabella had.

He swore with quiet venom.

So, yes, he might be *managing*. He might be maintaining some semblance of a normal and independent life. But it wasn't of any kind normality *he* recognised.

'Hi.'

She spoke quietly, but, momentarily distracted, Orlando felt the knife slip slightly and cursed again under his breath.

'I didn't hear you come in.'

'I didn't want to disturb you.'

Orlando felt anger rising inside him like acrid smoke.

It's a bit late for that.

Hesitantly she came a little further into the room, and he could see that she had changed into something dark—the same sweater and jeans she had been wearing this morning, maybe? 'I couldn't find you. The kitchen was the last place I thought of looking.'

'Really. Why's that?'

'I just thought that with a house like this you must have millions of staff. A chauffeur and a butler and all that—at the very least a cook.'

'No.'

His voice was sharp, and as if realising this he took a deep breath and dragged a hand through his hair. When he spoke again his tone was slightly softer, but he still gave the impression of making a huge effort to be polite. 'I have a housekeeper who comes in daily, and is in charge of a team of people who look after the house, and I employ a lot of people on the estate. But other than that, no. I chose to live here precisely because I wanted to be alone.'

Rachel came to a standstill in the centre of the room. He seemed to have placed an invisible exclusion zone around himself. *Keep away.*

'In that case I'm sorry to intrude on you like this.' Her voice was quiet, the emotion rigidly controlled. 'It's all such a nightmare, and I can't quite get my head around what I've done, but I can see now how awkward it is for you too.'

'You need to let someone know that you're safe,' he said curtly.

Rachel felt a small glow of surprise at his thoughtfulness. 'I have. I phoned earlier and left a message.' No need to mention that it had been on her own answer service at her agent's office, and that after she'd done it she'd dropped her phone out of the window and heard it crash into the shrubbery below.

'Good. The last thing I want is an irate fiancé turning up and accusing me of abduction.'

The glow was abruptly extinguished. 'Don't worry,' she said stiffly. 'If I could just stay for tonight, first thing in the morning I'll…go.'

Orlando clenched his fingers around the knife, steeling himself against the reproachful whispers of his conscience.

'Fine. As I said before, there's plenty of room. Just don't be surprised if you're left to yourself—I've got a lot on at work at the moment.'

'Of course not. What kind of work?'

'I have a private defence consultancy business, advising the MoD on all aspects of air defence,' he said with an edge of sarcasm. 'I also run the Easton estate and all its subsidiary companies. Would you like to see my CV?'

Rachel felt the colour rush to her cheeks as she realised she'd strayed too far into forbidden territory. And been warned off.

'I'm sorry,' she muttered. 'I ask too many questions. It comes of spending far too long on my own. I'm insatiably curious about— Oh God, Orlando—you're bleeding.'

For only a second did he falter, suddenly aware of the stickiness on his fingers. It must have happened when she'd come in to the kitchen and distracted him.

'It's nothing.'

'It's not! There's blood everywhere!'

Orlando glanced down. It was easy to see the bright flowering of red against the pale marble slab. Without a word he crossed to the sink and held his fingers under the tap. Jaw tensed, he kept his eyes fixed straight ahead.

Hesitantly Rachel came to stand beside him. 'Please, let me see. There's so much blood—it must be a deep cut.'

'It's fine,' he said savagely, but even he could see that the water swirling into the sink was deep pink. Too pink. Gritting his teeth, he kept his hand beneath the freezing stream of water.

He felt her fingers brush against his wrist. Warm, whisper-soft and infinitely tender, they closed around it and slowly drew his hand away from the tap.

For a moment Rachel felt him stiffen, and she thought he was going to snatch his hand away from her. Head tilted back, his eyes burned into hers with that angry intensity that betrayed the heat beneath his glacial exterior. She felt her stomach contract with that same powerful kick of emotion she had experienced upstairs as, for a shivering second, their gazes locked.

Tearing her eyes, from his she looked down at his hand. On the tips of both his index and middle fingers the blood welled darkly, and as she watched it fell in glistening beads which shattered on the pale stone floor. She sucked in a breath and bent her head, ashamed of her sudden urge to press her lips to his upturned palm. Wincing, she ran her thumb over the clean slice in the skin on his first finger.

It was deep.

His face was like stone, betraying not the faintest hint of emotion as the blood ran into her hand, dripping between her fingers onto the floor.

'We need to stop the bleeding,' she said weakly.

She looked up at him. He seemed a long way away, towering over her, scowling darkly...

He swore abruptly, succinctly, and Rachel felt his hands on her shoulders, guiding her backwards and pushing her into a chair, pressing her head down onto her knees. Then, holding the blood-soaked hand aloft, he turned away and in one swift movement pulled his shirt over his head. Bunching the soft cotton in one hand, he attempted to twist it around his damaged fingers.

The roaring in her ears gradually subsided, and Rachel lifted her head. Instantly she felt dizzy again. He was standing a few feet away with his back to her.

His *bare* back.

Breathlessly, helplessly, she let her eyes wander over the broad expanse of silken skin gleaming in the harsh spotlights, the ripple of taut muscles beneath it. Suddenly she could see exactly where that aura of barely concealed strength and power came from.

He was like a jungle animal—raw, physical, finely honed. But here, in this dark house, this sterile kitchen, it was as if he was caged.

Wounded.

Damaged.

One question filled her head. *Why?*

Dazedly she watched him make for the door, and half-stood. 'Orlando—I'm sorry. Is there anything I can do to help?'

The look he cast her was one of icy disdain. 'Sure. Finish cooking dinner.'

Shakily she opened the door of the vast, state-of-the-art fridge and stood motionless for long moments, clinging to the cool steel as she waited for normality to reassert itself.

Nothing looked remotely familiar, she thought dimly, gathering up what looked like a forlorn bunch of bloomless flowers, some slim greenish wands, some lumpen, unpromising-looking root vegetables. It was as if she'd been transported from Planet Normal to some alternative universe where everything was different.

Where a glance could make you tremble—not from fear, but with longing.

Where a touch could make you shiver—not with revulsion, but ecstasy…

She was suddenly aware that she'd come to a standstill in the middle of the kitchen, her arms full of produce. This was totally ridiculous, she thought wildly, giving herself a hard mental shake. Her life was in turmoil, and all she could do was fantasise about a man she hardly knew.

A man she hardly knew who was expecting her to cook dinner for him.

As if waking from a trance, she looked down at the bizarre items in her arms and let out a small exhalation of outrage. What was she thinking of? What the hell was she supposed to do with all this stuff? She was a pianist, for God's sake—a highly trained professional whose hands were exceptionally precious instruments, insured for thousands of pounds. She didn't *cook*…

Tossing her hair back from her face, she marched defiantly across to the island unit, intending to deposit the stupid green stuff and hunt down a takeaway menu instead. But as she approached she felt herself falter. The precariously balanced armful of ingredients slipped and tumbled onto the worktop, rolling to the floor as she saw the crimson pool of Orlando's blood still on the marble slab.

She stopped dead. And then stepped closer, stretched out a hand, and trailed her finger slowly through the dark red. She looked at her finger, at the glossy bead of his blood shining on its tip, as dark and precious as a ruby. There was something agonisingly intimate about it.

His blood.

The essence of him.

A shudder rippled through her.

'Everything all right?'

Orlando's voice from the doorway startled her from her thoughts, sent her hand flying to her throat in terror and confusion and shame.

'Yes…yes, of course.'

He came forward, dressed in a faded checked shirt, two fingers of his left hand bound up with gauze. 'You don't seem to have got very far.'

'No.' Making a conscious effort to steady her breathing, she lifted her chin and met his eye. 'I'm still clearing up. And I'm afraid I have no idea where to start with this. I've never cooked anything in my life, I don't know how to—'

He cut her off with a sharp, scornful sound. 'Then it's high time you learned.'

Rachel swallowed hard. Reaching for a cloth, she briskly wiped up the blood from the chopping board and shook her head. 'No. I'm no good at things like that….practical things.'

He gave a curse of pure, undisguised exasperation. OK, so Arabella might have been something of an *über*-achiever, but this girl seemed to take the word *incompetent* to a whole new level.

'What on earth makes you say that?' he said scathingly.

'How about twenty-three years of experience?' she retorted hotly. 'Or should that be twenty-three years of *in*experience? I've never done anything remotely domesticated!'

He couldn't see her toss her head, but he could certainly imagine it from the indignant tone of her voice, and maybe a little from the rustle of her heavy hair. Turning his mind resolutely from the mental images that instantly flared into life, he smothered a sneer.

'So now's your chance.' He picked up the knife. 'Come here.'

'No!'

Orlando froze. There was no mistaking the genuine anguish in her voice. For a long moment neither of them moved. He suddenly felt very, very tired.

'What are you afraid of?' he asked heavily, and then he remembered he was still holding the knife. 'Jeez, Rachel, I'm not going to hurt you for God's sake…!'

'I didn't think you were,' she whispered. 'It's just…' How could she explain that it wasn't that kind of fear, the fear of harm, that was causing her to tremble so violently, but fear of losing control. How could she explain that when she could hardly understand it herself?

He sighed. 'Come and stand here…'

Tentatively she took a step towards him, stopping a few feet away so he had to take her hand and draw her forwards. Gently, firmly, he positioned her in front of the marble chopping board and replaced the pepper he'd started to slice. She wondered if he could feel the frantic beat of her heart throbbing through her body, vibrating in the tiny space that separated them.

'Now…take hold of the pepper,' he said tonelessly. He was standing right behind her, and his voice close to her ear made a shiver run through her. She picked up the pepper in one shaking hand, holding onto it as if it was her last connection with reality.

'Good. Now, in the other hand pick up the knife.' His tone was carefully blank, but she could sense the tightly controlled frustration behind his words. Biting her lip in shame, she picked up the knife, watching the blade quiver in her uncertain grip until Orlando's hand closed over hers.

She gasped.

His arms encircled her, safe, strong, and she had to muster every inch of self-control she had to prevent her from leaning back into his embrace and letting her head fall on to his chest.

'No, I *can't*!'

She dropped the knife with a clatter and clenched her fists. Instantly he stepped backwards, and she turned round in time to see his uninjured hand go to his head, his fingers raking through his hair in a gesture of wordless exasperation.

'I'm sorry…' she said lamely. 'It's just…it's my hands. I have to be careful. They're…precious…'

He suddenly went very still.

'Precious?'

For a moment she watched as he half-raised his own hands, gazing downwards at them, at the fingers of the left one held rigidly in place by the bloodstained gauze. And then he turned away.

Precious. God, her shallowness took his breath away. *Her* hands were precious. Jeez.

She was unreal. His hands… His hands weren't just precious, they were his lifeline. This spoiled little girl would never understand that.

Not that he had any intention of her finding out.

CHAPTER FOUR

RACHEL'S eyes snapped open, and for a moment she felt suffocating fear as she stared into black nothingness. Her hands were twisted in the soft duvet, her fingers cramped, and the darkness was filled with the sickening thud of her heart.

Whimpering quietly, she unravelled her hands from the bedcovers and held them out in front of her as her eyes gradually adjusted to the gloom. She had dreamed of Carlos—a bizarre, terrible dream, where he chased her down a labyrinth of narrow lanes in her wedding dress, a knife flashing in his hand. And she knew with the terrible certainty that came in sleep that he intended to damage her hands with it, in revenge for humiliating him.

And then suddenly Orlando was there, naked to the waist and standing between her and Carlos, shielding her, until the next thing she knew her wedding dress was scarlet with his blood. All she could do was hold his lacerated hands, knowing as the blood kept flowing that she had brought this on him.

Earlier on in the kitchen she had felt dizzy as his bare chest had been revealed…too shocked and too shy to take in what she was seeing. But while her conscious mind had been having a fit of the vapours it seemed her eyes had missed nothing—noting every muscle, every sinew, every inch of delicious flesh. And they had chosen the dead hours of the night to revisit them all in disturbing detail.

Her pulse raced, and her body twitched and throbbed with

strange, uncomfortable sensations. In the thick silence she could hear nothing but the thudding of her heart.

Until her stomach gave a deafening rumble.

The sound broke the spell and made her laugh out loud with relief. Of course—she'd eaten virtually nothing all day, which totally explained the bizarre feelings that buzzed through her nerve-endings.

She was hungry, that was all. So hungry.

She had no idea what time it was, but food suddenly seemed like an imperative. She longed for the normality of hot buttered toast or a cup of tea. God, a chocolate biscuit seemed like the most desirable thing in the entire world…

Apart from Orlando Winterton's chest. And his sinuous back. And his green, green eyes…

No! Resolutely she swung her legs out of bed and strode to the door.

It was bitterly, bitterly cold, but she kept going, too nervous and jumpy to want to take the time to retrace her steps and retrieve her clothes. Silver light flooded the corridor, and passing window after window she saw a full moon, swathed in diaphanous drifts of cloud trailing languidly across the star-spiked sky. Rachel slipped noiselessly down the stairs and stopped, suddenly disorientated and wishing she had paid more attention earlier, instead of concentrating on Orlando Winterton's bloody hands…

Bloody hands. The words made images she was trying to forget come flooding back, and again she experienced that painful fizz inside her, as if someone had just pressed an electrode to her heart.

Blindly she stumbled in what she thought was the right direction for the kitchen. But there were so many doors. She opened one door and hesitated on the threshold, trying to get her bearings. The room was huge—surely running the whole length of one side of the house—and in the silver-blue shadows nothing looked familiar. The walls were high and dark—possibly black—the furniture a mixture of beautiful antiques and startlingly modern pieces. But all of this faded into the background as her eye was drawn to a curved bay window in the middle.

In it, bathed in moonlight as if spotlit on a stage, stood a piano. A grand piano.

Without thinking she found herself crossing the room towards it on cold, silent feet, tentatively reaching out a finger and running it gently down the keys, so that a soft rattle was the only sound that resulted. They felt smooth, solid, expensive…everything that a good piano should be.

She let her finger come to rest on Middle C. And pressed.

The sound was rich and mellow, and it flowed right through her, reverberating against her tautly stretched nerves. Her stomach tightened, but her hunger was forgotten. Suddenly all that mattered was this instrument and the need to lose herself in its exquisite familiarity. Heedless of the biting cold, she sat down, placing her bare feet on the chill metal pedals, letting her fingers rest deliciously on the keys for a second and closing her eyes in relief.

After a day of confusion, this, at last, was something she could understand and control. This was her way of interpreting the world, expressing emotion—the only way she had ever been shown and the only way she knew.

The moonlight turned her hands a bloodless blue as they began very quietly, very tentatively, to play. Without thinking she found the piece that was flowing from her fingers was Chopin's *Nocturne in E Minor*, its haunting notes flooding the night and filling her head with memories.

Memories she hadn't allowed to surface before, but suddenly wouldn't be suppressed any longer.

Closing her eyes, she gave in to them. Gradually she became aware that the keys were slippery with wetness and she realised she was crying, her tears dripping down onto her hands. She played on, not feeling the cold.

Compared to the ice inside her, it was nothing.

* * *

Sitting at his desk in the library, Orlando rubbed a hand over his tired eyes and leaned back in his chair. Apart from the soft red glow of the dying fire, the computer screen in front of him was the only source of light in the massive room, and he had been looking at it for too long. His eyes stung.

Thankfully, much of his business was conducted internationally, so the long hours of the night when sleep would often evade him could be usefully spent working. His computer was state-of-the-art, fitted with the very latest in screen-reading software, which he had always refused to use, preferring instead to type by touch and magnify the words to a size that made it possible for him to read them.

Technically.

Tonight they seemed to slide across the edges of his vision and dissolve without penetrating his mind.

The Middle Eastern border situation he was dealing with was balanced on a knife-edge. Hired as a consultant on aerial tactics and weapons deployment by the government, he was monitoring the situation on an hour-by-hour basis, grimly holding out against sending planes into an area where they had about as much chance of surviving as a pheasant over the Easton beech woods in shooting season.

As he knew all too well. It had been on a similar raid that Felix had been shot down. Or that was the supposition: they'd never even recovered his plane.

Sighing, Orlando got up and went to stand at one of the long windows, feeling a gust of cold air as he pulled back the curtain and looked out. Around the relentless blackness in the centre of his vision he could see the courtyard was bathed in moonlight.

With something that felt almost like a physical blow he recalled Felix's kindness that last time when he'd come home on leave, at the time when Andrew Parkes had given Orlando his diagnosis. Felix had accepted it with resignation, and for the remainder of his leave had treated Orlando with a horrible gentleness bordering on respect. When he had said goodbye it had almost as if he knew it would be the last time.

He'd had no intention of their relationship carrying on as before, Orlando realised now. As far as Felix had been concerned, if Orlando wasn't the big brother he could compete with and look up to, he was no brother at all. Nothing.

Orlando leaned back against the wooden shutter, tipping his head back and banging it softly, rhythmically, against the paneling. The pain reminded him that he was still alive. Sometimes he felt that he was disappearing, that just as the world was fading before his eyes, so he was fading from the eyes of the world.

Somewhere in the distance he could hear music. Maybe he'd finally lost it? he thought with savage desolation, striding to the door and pulling it open.

But he hadn't imagined it. Music was rippling through the dark rooms of the sleeping house, filling the empty spaces with sweet, sad resonance. With emotion. With life.

In the doorway of the grand salon he stopped, his breath catching in his throat. The effect of the music in the moonlit stillness was profound—it vibrated through him, smashing down defences he had spent the last year building. The room was ink-black washed with silver, and he turned his head, so that at the edge of his vision he could see her.

She had her back to him, her head tilted up so that her glowing red hair cascaded down over the thin slip of pale silk she was wearing. He could see with startling clarity the gleam of her bare shoulder in the moonlight, the shadowed drape of silk at the narrow part of her waist, just before it swelled out into sumptuous fullness. Hungrily, helplessly, his eyes sought her, desperate for more; but, as always, the instant he looked directly at her she disappeared into the black vortex in the centre of his vision. He felt his hands ball into fists of frustration as the music tugged invisible chords inside him, reawakening the feelings and needs he strove so hard to annihilate.

He was hardly aware of crossing the room, was conscious

only of the thudding of blood in his veins beneath the soaring swell of music that was flowing with perfect fluency and exquisite grace from her fingertips.

Her *precious* fingertips.

He felt a moan of realisation escape him. Oh, God. He'd been so wrapped up in himself that he hadn't given her a chance to explain what she'd meant. He'd thought she was some silly, pampered princessy type, who didn't want to damage her false nails, but she was a *pianist*…

Remorse and self-loathing stole through him. His bandaged fingers throbbed and ached as he gripped the table beside him, waiting for this unwelcome, stinging insight into the man he had become to subside.

The music filled his head, each lovely, liquid note echoing inside the empty spaces of his heart. Until he noticed, above the piano, another sound.

An inhalation. A soft, swift gasp of indrawn breath.

He waited a few seconds. And heard another. The girl sitting a few feet away from him was creating that miraculous, moving music while crying her heart out very quietly.

He didn't want to go to her. He wanted to leave the room and go back to his study and his work. He wanted to wall himself up again, pack his heart in ice and put his needs, his desires, back in the past.

He wanted all of that, and still he found himself going towards her. It felt as if he was crawling over broken glass, but he couldn't stop.

Playing the last heartbreaking bars, Rachel closed her eyes and let her head drop backwards as the tears coursed down her cheeks.

Why had she played this piece?

It was the dream, perhaps, that had brought it all back. This was the piece she had played that horrible night at Carlos's apartment in Vienna, when he had forced himself on her for the first time. They had been engaged for about three weeks, and, coming back from dinner in a restaurant, her mother had pleaded a headache and gone straight to the hotel. There had been no question of arguing when Carlos had suggested she went with him to his beautiful penthouse for a nightcap, and she had done as she was told without demur. Just as she always had.

Until…

Until later. When she had felt his hands, damp and insistent, sliding up beneath her blouse as she'd played the Chopin. And then she had protested and fought with all her strength.

A sob escaped her.

Just at that moment she felt warm hands on her shoulders, sliding down her chilled arms to cradle her from behind. Letting out a cry, she stumbled to her feet, desperate to get away as her mind, made irrational by the terrible memories, made instant, impossible connections. Stepping away from the piano stool, she whirled round, adrenalin giving her movements an intense energy.

Orlando stepped back, holding up his hands. His face was entirely in shadow.

'It's you' she whispered, relief coursing through her. 'It's *you*.'

'Who did you think?'

She shook her head, looking away, feeling suddenly foolish and ashamed. Ashamed of the person Carlos had turned her into. 'I wasn't thinking properly…I was just…frightened. Of the dark. Does that sound stupid?'

He gave a low, mirthless laugh. 'No. Not at all.' He took a step towards her, into a square of moonlight falling through the huge windows, and it painted silver streaks in his black hair and shimmered on the hard planes of his lean face. 'You were crying.'

'Yes… It's ridiculous, but you were right. I totally lack courage in everything. I'm afraid all the time…'

She stopped as he reached out and lifted her right hand in his. Mesmerised, she watched as he looked down at it with his strange intense stare, turning it palm upwards and unfolding her fingers with a sweep of his thumb, as if he were spreading the petals of a flower. And then he placed his own damaged, bandaged hand over hers, and Rachel closed her eyes, unable to control the series of seismic shocks that juddered up her arm and into some locked-up, secret part of her. Her hands had always been her way of expressing herself, through the music that they created, but never had they brought her this kind of feeling. She felt as if she held a tornado.

'That's OK,' he said bleakly. 'It's OK to be afraid. It's how you deal with it that matters.'

Looking downwards, he could see the paleness of her skin against his. In the moonlight she was so white, like porcelain, and he found himself wondering whether, given the colour of her hair, she also had freckles that he couldn't see. He wanted to raise her hand to his lips, to feel the coolness of her flesh against his face and breathe in the clean, young scent of her. He let his bandaged hand fall to his side, but somehow his other hand remained pressed against hers, palm to palm. Her fingers were almost as long as his, though finer. But as they meshed with his he could feel their incredible strength.

She moved towards him until she could almost feel the electric current crackling in the small space that separated them.

'But I'm tired of being afraid. I want to be brave.'

She sounded both wistful and angry, and the words seemed to resonate in the charged air for a second. Then, her eyes never leaving his, she moved closer, closing the gap between their tense bodies, and stood on tiptoe to brush her lips against his in a gossamer-light kiss.

'Show me how to be brave,' she murmured.

His answer was a low curse as he captured her trembling mouth with a kiss of ferocious intensity. The miracle of his touch on Rachel's skin seared a path of purifying fire through the confusion and revulsion Carlos's touch had left in its wake. Suddenly, in the arms of this man, everything that had scared and confused her seemed so simple and so beautiful. One hand was still holding his, their fingers locked, but she lifted the other to his face, feeling the hard planes of his stubble-roughened cheek beneath her palm, feeling the leanness of his jaw as he kissed her with a passion and purpose that made the past irrelevant. His hand was in the small of her back, moving upwards and coming to rest between her shoulderblades, holding her against him with a touch so light it was almost as if he was afraid to crush her.

'Rachel…No.'

Orlando pulled away, his fingers still entwined with Rachel's, until he was holding her at arm's length. He knew he was a hair's breadth from surrendering control, but the lure of oblivion was incredibly powerful. To be, for a few blissful minutes, the man he used to be—powerful, capable, in command, omnipotent.

But he wouldn't use her for that.

'Please…'

She had her face tilted up to his, so that he could feel the warmth of her sweet breath fanning his cheek. She was shivering, and he could hear the yearning in her voice.

'You don't need this.'

With monumental self-control he turned, running a hand through his hair as his gut twisted with desire and agonising frustration. He felt as if he had been kicked repeatedly in the stomach.

'I do. Oh, God, Orlando, you don't know how much I need this. Please…' She was almost sobbing with longing.

He didn't turn, feeling his hands clench into fists, until the pain in his lacerated fingers provided a welcome distraction from his tortured conscience.

The last thing he wanted was a relationship, complications… companionship, for God's sake. He wanted to be left alone with his suffering and his pain.

But, sweet Lord above, he wanted her. Wanted to lose himself in her. Now. Right now.

Silently she had slipped through the shadows to stand in front of him, a pale, trembling moon goddess. He stared straight ahead, but in the moonlight he could see the silvery glisten of tears on her cheeks.

'I need you.'

Her whispered words broke down his last defence. With a moan of despair he gathered her into his arms and brought his mouth down onto her soft lips, feeling as well as hearing her answering moan of relieved surrender.

He could feel the frenzied pounding of her heart inside her shaking body. She seemed so scared, so vulnerable and needy, that his arms tightened around her, cradling her against the hard length of his body in an instinctive effort to warm and protect her. It felt so good. Her hands cupped his face, then slid to twine around his neck, her strong fingers massaging the base of his skull, pushing him downward, deepening the kiss, until his head was filled with nothing but the taste of her and the feel of her slender young body beneath the silky nightdress.

Reality melted away, and with it the demons and black dogs of despair. There was nothing now but darkness—a blissful darkness that only accentuated the powerful, miraculous sensations that were exploding inside him. Lifting his mouth from Rachel's, he buried his face in her fragrant hair.

'If we don't stop this now, I won't be able to.'

'Good.'

Her voice was low and fierce. *Carnal*, he thought, at the very moment when he felt her hands at his waist, slipping beneath his shirt and moving over the taut flesh of his stomach. All further thought became impossible.

Rachel felt his shuddering exhalation of breath in her hair as her trembling fingers fumbled with his belt. She was no longer shivering with cold, but with excitement. With heat.

At the beginning her overwhelming need had been to have the stain of Carlos's touch washed from her skin, but at that moment she couldn't have said who Carlos was. There was no thought in her head but Orlando, and she needed nothing but the feeling of his hands on her waist, his lips against her hair, her ear, her neck…

His thumbs swept upwards over the quivering skin of her midriff to run along the sharp ridges of her ribs. She was lost inside his kiss, but felt him gently pushing her backwards as her hands finally released the top button of his trousers and slid downwards. And then the silence was broken by a discordant clash of notes as her bottom came to rest on the piano keyboard. She was tearing at the buttons of his shirt now, her mouth never leaving his as her hands hungrily sought the warmth of his skin, pushing the fabric down over his massive shoulders, feeling them bunch and flex under her questing fingers.

He was so huge. So powerful. Dazedly, she tore her mouth from his.

'I want to see you,' she whispered.

He looked down at her, *into* her. His face was utterly unreadable. The moonlight bleached his skin to an unearthly white, so that he looked like the ghost of some heroic centurion. Only the rise and fall of his broad chest and the dark glitter of his eyes gave away the fact that he was real.

'You're so beautiful,' she murmured in wonder.

He didn't smile. With an expression of intense concentration he moved towards her again, and caught hold of the hem of her nightdress in his hands, drawing it slowly upwards over her head until she stood in front of him, spread against the piano, completely naked. His head jerked backwards as his hands slid upwards over the flat of her stomach, her arching ribs.

'So are you.'

The intensity of his voice sent a pulse of liquid need crashing through her, which was nothing to the deranging impulses that sizzled through her central nervous system as he cupped her breasts in his hands, shifting her weight backwards onto the piano. With another decadent, dissonant chord, she opened her legs and pulled him towards her.

It wasn't Chopin. It was a million times sweeter.

Their mouths found each other, and then he was lifting her, swinging her into his arms and carrying her across the room. For a second he lifted his mouth from hers, negotiating a path between the low mirrored table and the sofas, and then he lowered her gently to the floor.

She gasped as she felt soft, warm fur against her bare skin, twining her fingers luxuriously into it as she raised herself up and let her head fall backwards, arching her back as his lips traced a path of bliss down the column of her throat. She caught the back of his head, pulling him downwards, harder, until they were both lying in the thick fur, their mouths devouring each other, bruising, biting, tasting.

No moonlight penetrated their dark intimacy. The world was reduced to the sensations of the flesh. Abandoning his strait-jacket of self-control, Orlando was lost in the feel of her hair in his hands, her lips on his neck. She smelled of roses, the warm smell of summer and purity and beauty, and as he entered her it was like regaining paradise.

She was exquisite. He heard her soft, throaty gasp and felt her clutch at his back, her strong fingers pressing into his skin, urging him deeper, demanding all of him, as she raised her legs and wrapped them around his waist, gripping him, cherishing him. And then her hands were cupping his face, imprisoning it milli-metres from her own as her mouth captured his again, and he felt it open in a cry of high, primeval release.

She stiffened, and for a second was completely still, before he felt her shudder with ecstasy in his arms. It was too much. Helplessly he plunged headlong into blissful release, and as he did so the relentless, smothering blackness in his head was lit up with dazzling explosions of red and green and gold.

CHAPTER FIVE

'I CAN see angels.'

Rachel lay beside him, gazing upwards, and her voice was soft and drowsy and sated.

'Does that mean I've died and gone to heaven?'

Orlando stirred, rolling over to face her and propping himself up on one elbow. He could hear the smile in her words and wished he could look into her face. He wanted to kiss the corners of that smile and make it fade into something more intense and abstract as his lips moved further down her body. He wanted to see if that astonishing passion of hers lit up her eyes, made her skin glow…

But he couldn't.

'I doubt it, if I'm here too,' he said harshly. There was no peace and light in the place *he* inhabited.

'Don't say that,' she whispered softly. 'You saved me today. For that, if nothing else, you've earned your place in heaven.'

She pulled him down beside her again, sweeping her arm upwards in a wide arc, and then he understood. Remembered. He'd forgotten the carved plasterwork on the ceiling above them, and how at night the charcoal-grey-painted background seemed to recede into the darkness, making the angels depicted there come alive. He'd loved it as a child. But he'd stopped looking at it long before he'd stopped being able to see it.

'Look,' she murmured. 'They're so beautiful. I can't imagine that heaven could be any better than this, can you?'

Orlando sighed. Of course he saw nothing. The colours that had filled his head as he'd exploded inside her had faded, leaving a deeper darkness—like an empty winter sky after the fireworks were all finished.

'I can't imagine heaven exists at all,' he said with quiet brutality. There was no such thing as eternal bliss. All joy was fleeting, and came at a price. He had allowed himself this wonderful, unexpected release. But now it was over, and it was time to retreat to the safety of his walls of ice and steel.

In the velvet darkness he felt her hand against his face and tensed against the tenderness in her touch.

'Oh, Orlando, were you always so cynical?'

'No.'

'What happened? Was it Felix?'

He caught her hand, enclosing it in his, feeling the bones and sinews beneath the soft skin—feeling both her fragility and her incredible, surprising strength.

'Maybe.' The injustice that his brother's life—a useful, courageous life—had been extinguished while he was left to struggle on endlessly in a worthless one. That had made him cynical. 'There were other things too.'

'Tell me,' she breathed.

He dropped a kiss into her palm, curling her long fingers around it as if he were saying goodbye.

'No.' He got up in one lithe movement and reached for his clothes. 'There's nothing to tell. I lost something, that's all. Something I took for granted. And now I miss it. All the bloody time.'

Especially now. Especially right this moment, when I would give anything to be able to see you…

He turned away and, suddenly aware of how cold it was, reached up onto the high marble mantelpiece to feel for a box of matches. The kindling in the fireplace caught straight away and he straightened up, watching the small, brave flicker of flame take hold of the darkness.

Behind him, Rachel sat up slowly, tucking her knees up in front of her and resting her chin on them. 'You told me that it's OK to be afraid—that it's how you deal with it that counts.'

Orlando said nothing.

'I think the same could be said of loss. You can't change it. But you can deal with it.'

He gave a low, bitter laugh. 'You think so?'

His coldness took her by surprise. Suddenly she was aware that she was naked, and she felt foolish and exposed. It was as if the closeness that they had just shared had never existed. The barriers had gone back up.

'I'm sorry...I don't know anything about it. I'm a pianist, not a psychologist,' she muttered, getting up and looking around for her discarded nightdress.

He turned slowly round to face her, moonlight silvering his devastating, chilly face, firelight gilding his massive shoulders. Once again she was reminded of some gladiatorial warrior from mythology, and she wondered what had hurt him so badly. What—or whom.

'Why didn't you tell me you were a pianist before? I didn't understand about your hands—I thought you were being vain.'

He heard her soft exhalation. 'I don't know...maybe I thought you'd know. Some people do, you know—recognise me. Carlos's PR people did a huge poster campaign for my first CD.'

And in that instant, in a flash as bright, as dazzling as the glowing colours he'd seen earlier, he saw in his mind's eye the girl in the picture that day outside Andrew Parkes' office. Realisation hit him like the lash of a whip—sudden and shocking.

'I'm a philistine,' he said bluntly, turning back to the fire. 'I hardly ever leave this place—I'm far too wrapped up in work. The last time I attended a musical recital was in the officers' mess; it featured songs that I hope you've never heard, and it ended with the piano having petrol poured over it and being set alight.'

Rachel gasped. 'No! Why?'

'It's an RAF tradition. It happens every year.'

'But that's terrible! How could you bear to do it?'

He looked into the flames. 'It's just a piano,' he said simply, and the implications of his words seemed to drift and settle in the moonlit room.

'You're right. I forget. Sometimes I feel like it's my only friend.' She wrapped her arms tightly around herself and made an attempt at a laugh. 'In fact, let's face it, it is my only friend. I think it really hit me this afternoon, when I was all alone in that room, waiting to be taken to the church, that the only good relationship I've ever had in my life has been with the piano.'

Her loneliness was palpable. Orlando was struck by the irony: he had spent the last year brutally trying to shut out the outside world, while this girl was reaching out to it. He felt the ice around his frozen heart crack open a little.

'What brought you here? To a tiny place in the middle of nowhere like Easton?' He had to make an effort to keep the frustration out of his voice, but he needed to ask the question. Why had fate brought her here, to scrape the tender flesh off scars that were still healing, still hurting?

She sank back down onto the fur rug and pulled her knees up again, wrapping her arms protectively around them. 'Carlos's PR people found The Old Rectory, and thought it would be the perfect place for the wedding. Very English, very quietly grand—which all fitted in with the brand they created for me. They took out a six-month lease on it, but until the day before yesterday I'd never seen it. It could have been anywhere.'

The fire stretched long fingers of warmth into the room and painted her skin in peach and gold. Orlando had heard about the brain compensating for what the eye couldn't see, but until now he had never experienced it, or believed it was possible. But in that instant he could picture vividly the sadness in her amber eyes, the gentle swell of her upper lip, her delicate chin.

She got up slowly and walked towards him, her head bent so that the firelight made her hair glow like vintage cognac. Standing beside him, she pressed a hand against his chest, over his heart.

'I'm so glad it wasn't anywhere else,' she said with quiet ferocity. 'I'm so glad it was here.'

He took a deep breath and very gently moved her hand, turning away to spare her from reading the truth on his face; the selfish, hateful truth that he wished she'd never come into his life and smashed up the fragments he'd been painstakingly piecing together again. But then his attention was suddenly drawn away from her to a movement beyond, in the clear periphery of his vision. He walked towards the window, where the piano stood bathed in blue light.

Behind him Rachel stood, washed in fire-gold and spilling out warmth and softness. In front of him was a featureless waste-land of white.

He felt his lips twitch into a smile of irony as the symbolism hit him.

'It's snowing.'

'Oh…' She came to stand beside him, staring out in wonder at the enchanted garden. Snow already lay like icing on the clipped box spheres, making them look like fat cupcakes, and it had turned the bare branches of the trees into elaborate confections of spun sugar which sparkled in the moonlight. It was like a scene from *The Nutcracker* ballet. 'It's lovely…you're so lucky to live in such a gorgeous place…'

He smiled, and it was as cold and beautiful as the silvered winter garden in front of them. Goosebumps rose on her arms and a shiver rippled through her.

'Let's just say it's rather wasted on me.'

He stooped to pick up her nightdress from where it had been thrown, down by the piano, and untangled it, holding it out ready to slip over her head. Obedient as a child, she raised her arms, suddenly feeling very, very tired.

'What time is it?'

'After three.'

She stifled a yawn as it suddenly occurred to her that he had still been dressed when he'd found her. 'But you were still up…'

'Working. And checking over the arrangements for tomorrow.'

'What's happening tomorrow?

He took her hand, pulling her gently towards the door. 'The annual Easton Ball, to mark the end of the shooting season. It's an old tradition.'

'Oh, how lovely…' Rachel's drowsy mind was instantly filled with pictures of ladies in beautiful swirling dresses, men in black tie….Orlando in black tie…

Orlando gave a dry laugh. 'Lovely? No. I can assure you it'll be like the seventh circle of hell. The estate still makes a large part of its revenue from pheasant shooting, mainly by organising shooting parties for groups from big corporations and finance houses in London, and they all come down here solely to prove how macho they are. Tomorrow night the house'll be full of drunken City boys determined to down as much champagne as possible and impress everyone with their lord-of-the-manor credentials.'

'And you have to organise this thing?'

They were out in the darkened hallway now. The snow had changed everything, making the shadows blue and giving the air a muffled sense of suspended time. Rachel faltered, flinching as her feet touched the ice-cold marble tiles, and in an instant Orlando had scooped her up into his arms and was carrying her towards the stairs. Her eyes were on a level with his. They were narrow, slanting, impenetrable.

'Not really. I employ caterers and a party planner, and my extremely capable housekeeper does the rest.'

Above her, Winterton ancestors scowled down through the ages and through the darkness as they passed

'It must be horrible to have your house overrun with strangers.'

'It's the first time I'll have done it on my own.' For two years Arabella had taken over the job, with obsessive attention to detail, and she had organised lavish themed occasions that had looked marvelous on the pages of *Hello!* but had intimidated the Easton locals deeply. 'Last year it was cancelled because it was right after Felix's death.'

Safe in his arms, Rachel let her head fall against his shoulder. She could feel the steady, soothing beat of his heart against her ribs and looked up, seeing the strong lines of his jaw, the sinuous column of his throat. Emotion she was too tired to analyse solidified in her chest.

'It'll be hard without him,' she murmured.

'Yes.' Briefly he glanced down at her, and smiled. 'Though the year before he caused an awful lot of trouble by disappearing upstairs with the wife of a hedge fund manager. I had to give the guy a crate of vintage port to keep the peace. At least I won't have that to worry about this year.'

Rachel felt a small stab of surprise. 'Really? I imagined Felix would be like you, but you must have been very different.'

'No. We were as bad as each other. It's just that as the oldest I always had the most to lose.'

They were at the top of the stairs now. No moonlight penetrated the courtyard beneath the windows, and the corridor was in deep shadow. Rachel's head fell back onto Orlando's chest. He stared straight ahead, trying not to think about how good she felt in his arms, how right.

Because it wasn't right. It was impossible.

'Don't you ever turn the light on?'

'I don't need to. I've lived here all my life. I know my way around this house with my eyes closed.'

That, after all, was one of the reasons he'd come back.

In the bedroom he laid her on the bed and folded the covers over her, then stood back abruptly, his arms falling to his sides. Already they felt empty.

Turning to go, he had ruthlessly to suppress the masochistic part of his brain that was at that moment taunting him with thoughts of how it would feel to lie down beside her and hold her against him through the freezing hours of darkness, to wake up with his cheek against her hair and know that that red, vibrant, living blaze of colour would be the first thing he would see.

One night…just one night…

The agonising irony of the situation hit him like a punch in the ribs, momentarily winding him. He wanted her. He wanted her and the terrible thing was that having her just now had made him want her all the more.

How very optimistic of him to think that once would be enough.

But he'd had his chance to be open and he hadn't taken it, and his punishment was knowing that everything that had just happened between them was based on a lie. He'd deceived her into thinking he was something and someone he could never be. The person she'd just made such glorious, abandoned love to was the old Orlando Winterton. The one who had died a year ago.

He had almost reached the door when she spoke.

'Thank you.' Her voice soft and heavy with sleep.

'What for?'

'For having me.' He heard a breath of drowsy laughter which seemed to caress him in the dark. 'Not like *that*. I mean, having me to stay. Although…' There was a pause. 'Actually…like *that* too…' Her voice was slowing. She was almost asleep 'It was the first…time…'

He froze, adrenaline and guilt and remorse hitting him like a tidal wave. 'The first time?' He crossed the room again, back to the bedside, where she lay perfectly still.

He reached out a hand, finding the velvet-soft skin of her cheek. 'The first time, Rachel? You were a virgin?'

She stirred and exhaled—deeply, contentedly. 'No. But…it was the first time…. I've ever wanted it.'

CHAPTER SIX

RACHEL ran lightly down the wide staircase, running her fingers through her wildly sleep-tousled hair as she went. As she'd hurried along the corridor upstairs she'd seen that the courtyard at the centre of the house lay under a covering of white as thick and luxurious as the goosedown duvet which she had slept beneath last night.

And had, in the end, slept wonderfully well. It was as if Orlando had hushed the storm that had been raging inside her for as long as she could remember. She felt...liberated.

She had escaped from Carlos, and in the process she had discovered herself. Maybe she wasn't the incompetent idiot it had always suited him and her mother to make her out to be. After all, he'd said she was frigid, and he'd certainly been wrong about that...

This particularly enticing train of thought was interrupted by the sudden shrill ring of a telephone, echoing through the silent house. Looking round, Rachel traced it to a table in the entrance hall, and hesitated, not knowing what to do. There was no sign of Orlando—but then might he be in his study and would pick it up there? She walked on a few steps, but the ringing continued in a way that seemed to Rachel to be getting increasingly urgent.

She turned and looked back at the phone nervously. She'd never had to answer the phone for anyone else before. In fact she'd hardly had any need to answer the phone at all...

Courage.

For goodness' sake—it was a telephone, not an explosive device, she told herself disgustedly and seized the receiver.

'Hello, Easton Hall?' Pride suffused her at her new-found competence. 'Can I help you?'

'Ohh…?' It was a woman's voice, smoky, drawling, surprised. Rachel felt the confidence of a few moments ago evaporate. 'That's not Mrs Harper, is it?'

'N-no.' Rachel stammered. 'Can I take a message?'

'Well…' said the woman, and the short word seemed to crackle with indignation—as if Rachel was personally responsible for Mrs Harper's absence and had organised it on purpose. 'Could I speak to Orlando, please?'

'Oh…I'm sorry but I don't think he's here,' Rachel said faintly. 'I mean, I've only just got up and I haven't seen—'

'*Got up?*' repeated the voice, in a tone of utter disbelief. 'I see. In that case I do apologise.' The woman gave an incredulous laugh. 'I assumed you were one of Mrs Harper's helpers…'

She left the sentence hanging, making Rachel feel compelled to rush into an explanation. 'No—no, I'm just a friend…of…of Orlando's…'

Rachel winced at the blatant cliché.

'A *friend*?'

The woman's voice was suddenly sharp with animosity, and Rachel held her breath, wondering whether she should just put the phone down now, before she incriminated herself even further. There was a long pause, but then the woman at the other end started speaking again, her voice suddenly syrupy with concern.

'In that case, as you're a *friend* of Orlando, I wonder if you could maybe just…tell me how he is?

Rachel swallowed, caught off-guard by this change of tack. 'He's…fine.'

There was a small sigh. 'I'm sorry. I know this must sound mad and you don't know me, but I don't know who else to ask. How is he *really*? I mean, as a *friend*? Does he seem miserable to you?'

Pieces of the jigsaw were flying into place with a speed that took Rachel's breath away. And her foolish, naïve happiness along with it. Her throat suddenly felt very dry. 'Yes,' she croaked. 'He seems miserable.'

'Oh, God…what a mess,' the woman said slowly. Her sexy, lightly accented voice was choked with emotion, and Rachel was ashamed of the strength of her hostility. She wanted to hurl the phone at the wall, as if that could somehow hurt the person at the other end. The person Orlando loved.

'But thank you,' continued the woman. 'It helps to know he's as unhappy as I am. It's mad that we're apart…you've told me all I've needed to hear to convince me to come back.'

'I'll tell him…' Rachel just managed to mutter through numb lips.

'No!' The response was instantaneous, and surprisingly sharp. 'No. Don't tell him. Don't say anything. I'd like to surprise him.' She gave a breathy, intimate laugh that contained no trace of any unhappiness at all. Only triumph.

Nauseous, Rachel was just replacing the receiver with a shaking hand when the front door was flung open. Orlando stood in the doorway, his broad shoulders blocking out the white glare behind him, snowflakes resting on his dark hair. He came towards her, a sharp line carved between his dark brows.

'Who was that?'

'She didn't give a name,' Rachel muttered, and jumped as the phone rang again. Orlando snatched it up instantly, his eyes blazing.

'Arabella?'

Rachel took a few stumbling steps backwards.

So that was it. She really should be grateful. It was far better to know before she made even more of a fool of herself than she had already.

Going into the kitchen, she tried to quell the biting sense of disappointment and hurt that burned in her chest. Last night had come with no promises, she had understood that perfectly, but she had at least wanted to be allowed to believe that for as long as it had lasted it had meant something.

The way he had looked at her—her throat constricted painfully as she remembered the intensity of his stare—the way he'd seemed to look beyond her face and into her soul. Now she understood why. *He hadn't seen her at all.*

He'd seen this Arabella. An image of a dark, exotic supermodel swathed in black satin sheets swam into Rachel's head as she mindlessly held the sleek designer kettle under the tap. She was just adding scarlet lipstick and a bottle of champagne to the image when she jumped back with a howl, as water sprayed copiously all over her.

Suddenly strong hands relieved her of the kettle and turned off the tap. Dripping and miserable, she looked up into Orlando's darkly scowling face and felt a further twist of pain.

'I was just going to have a cup of coffee, and then I'll go,' she muttered, not meeting his eye.

'Don't be ridiculous. Go where?'

He seemed distracted. Distracted and angry. And very cold. She felt her bruised heart shrivel a little.

'I don't know, exactly, but obviously I'll find a hotel or something. I have plenty of money…'

'No. You're not going anywhere.'

Orlando said the words as if it hurt him to speak them. It pretty much did. For the sake of his peace of mind he wanted her gone. For the sake of his conscience he needed her to stay. He wasn't quite sure what she'd meant by saying she'd never wanted sex before last night, but something about it troubled him deeply.

'But we agreed… It was just for last night.'

Abruptly Orlando moved away, going to stand at the other side of the kitchen with his back to her in a gesture which told her just as plainly as if he'd spoken the words out loud that as far as he was concerned *last night* was something he didn't wish to be reminded of.

'That was the housekeeper's son on the phone just now. He was ringing to say that Mrs Harper slipped on some ice on her way here this morning and is on her way to hospital now, with a suspected broken ankle and fractured collarbone.'

'Oh, poor her!'

'You're kinder than I am. My first reaction was far less self-less. Today of all bloody days.'

'The ball…of course.'

'Yes.' He didn't turn round.

He couldn't bear to look at her this morning, Rachel thought miserably.

'I want you to stay.'

The words cut through her thoughts, unexpected and shocking.

'What?'

He sighed, his huge shoulders rising and falling, his head drooping for a moment before he seemed to make a massive effort to conceal his exasperation and repeat the words.

'I said, I want you to stay.' He spoke through gritted teeth, with exaggerated patience, as if she were very stupid. 'I have to work. There's an incident brewing over border control in the Middle East, and I'm going to be in consultation with Whitehall and the Pentagon for most of the day. I need you…' He paused to suck in a breath. 'I need you to help tonight, and with getting everything ready.'

Rachel shook her head in bewilderment, trying to keep a grip on reality. For the briefest second she'd allowed herself to imagine that that pause after *I need you* meant something—that Orlando Winterton was asking her to stay because he wanted her, not because he was short-staffed.

'I can't—you know I can't! I'd be hopeless, Orlando. You know I'm completely impractical. I'd make a mess of it all, and spill red wine down someone's priceless designer dress or something…'

He spun round to face her, dragging a hand through his hair. His other hand, the bandaged fingers stained with blood, stayed limp at his side, and the sight of that small vulnerability made her heart skip a beat.

'Don't be ridiculous,' he snapped. 'There'll be caterers, for God's sake. I'm not asking you to be a *waitress*.'

The ice in his wintry eyes extinguished her flicker of compassion and left a smoulder of anger. 'Then what?' She raised her chin an inch, staring at him defiantly. 'If you don't want me to fill in as a waitress, what do you want, Orlando? A stand-in *mistress*?'

She stopped abruptly, heat and colour flooding into her cheeks as the absurdity of the word—of the accusation—sounded in her ears. *Mistress?* She sounded like a prim governess in a Victorian novel.

A smile spread across his face: slow, lazy, dangerously mesmerising.

'My *mistress*? No. I can assure you that there will be absolutely no need for you to take your duties that far, thank you. Though maybe it's just as well you mentioned it, so we can get things absolutely straight. I'm asking you to stay on for purely practical purposes, and whatever happened between us last night is completely irrelevant.'

Rachel bit back her gasp of hurt. 'And what if I don't want to stay?'

He shrugged, levering himself upright from where he had been lounging with deceptive indifference against the countertop, and took a couple of steps towards her.

'Then go. As soon as you've decided where. I'm asking for your help, not issuing a prison sentence.'

He was throwing her a lifeline. She knew that. Giving her time. So why was she hesitating?

She looked down at her hands. Subconsciously her fingers were stretching and flexing, getting ready for the two hours of practice she'd put in first thing in the morning in her old life. Her life with Carlos. The life she had run away from yesterday, with no thought of where she was going.

She shoved her hands into the pockets of her jeans and looked up at Orlando with a small, painful smile. Pride was a luxury she simply couldn't afford at the moment.

'Of course I'll stay,' she said in a subdued voice. 'Thank you. I'll make myself as useful as I can.'

He nodded curtly, his gaze brushing over her for a second, as cold and fleeting as snowflakes on her face. But then he turned and left the room, and it was like being abandoned in Siberia. Naked.

Orlando strode into the library and slammed the door.

The small act of violence made him feel slightly better for a second, before despair closed in on him again, cutting him off from the rest of the world. Like the snow, which was falling again outside in heavy, swirling flakes.

He ought to be proud of himself, he thought mockingly. For the first time in a year he'd done something selfless. Something altruistic. For the first time in the last twelve miserable, desperate, depressing months he had actually done something *heroic*.

And she'd reacted as if he'd asked her to embrace a boa constrictor.

Walking across to the desk, he felt his face contort into a grimace of self-disgust.

She couldn't wait to leave this morning. She had nowhere to go, but she was still planning to walk out of there. She could hardly boil a kettle, but she'd still decided she'd rather fend for herself than stay with him. Knives of pain shot through his damaged hand as it tightened convulsively into a fist.

Why?

Last night she had been different. He felt a moan of torment form in his throat as he remembered her softness, her compliance….her gratitude, for heaven's sake. And at the time he'd felt like the most callous bastard who'd ever walked, because he'd known he was going to have to let her down. This last minute role-reversal was unsettling and bewildering.

What had changed?

A thought crept in to the edge of his mind like a cockroach…unpleasant, and impossible to completely destroy.

Arabella.

Apart from his doctors, she was the only living person to know about his sight.

And she'd spoken to Rachel this morning.

Taking her coffee, Rachel wandered out into the hallway, feeling at a loss. In the distance she could hear the bangs and shouts of the teams of workers clearing the furniture in the long drawing room and setting up the tables in the dining room. The house felt so different today, when it was filled with noise and life. Last night—the moonlight, the silence, the snow—seemed to belong to a dream, unreachable and unreal.

She found herself standing in the doorway of the drawing room, although she couldn't remember consciously deciding to go there, and watched in a trance as two men with their shirt-sleeves rolled back lifted the last sofa and carried it out of the door at the far end.

The room was bare, except for the rug on the floor where Orlando had laid her, knelt over her as his hands had slipped over her body, trailing ecstasy as the angels above had looked down on them…

'Excuse me, you wouldn't happen to know where I could find Mrs Harper, would you?'

Rachel jumped. The voice at her elbow was incredibly well-bred, but decidedly frazzled. Turning round, she found herself looking into the face of a girl not much older than she was, but as different as it was possible to be. Sleek, elegant, sophisticated, she was the sort of girl you expected to see in the champagne bar of Harrods, surrounded by a group of matching friends called Henrietta and Lucinda.

She held out a beautifully manicured hand. 'Sorry, I'm Lucinda. From Ice and Fire? The party planners?'

'Oh—of course,' said Rachel, blushing. For a moment the name of Lucinda's business had thrown her. 'I'm Rachel. I'm terribly sorry, but Mrs Harper won't be coming today. She's slipped on the ice and broken her ankle.'

In sympathy with Mrs Harper, Lucinda's face fell. 'Oh, knickers,' she wailed. 'This sodding weather! I was *so* counting on having someone to help. Half of our office are in bed with hellish flu, which means I've come on my own. I had to set off at some perfectly indecent hour, and I've had the most nightmarish journey—'

She was interrupted by a loud blast of Handel's *Firework Music* from her huge designer handbag, and, glancing apologetically at Rachel, plucked out her mobile. As she turned away to speak into it Rachel had the chance to admire the exquisite cut of her black trouser suit, her shiny pale pink nails with their bright white tips. She looked capable and professional, Rachel thought enviously, pulling the sleeves of her beloved but decidedly distressed cashmere jumper down over her own plain hands.

With a vivid curse that was entirely at odds with the cut-glass tones in which it was spoken, Lucinda threw the phone back into her bag and turned to Rachel. 'That was the florist,' she said miserably. 'All the flights out of the Channel Islands have been grounded this morning, so the flowers won't be here.'

Rachel's heart went out to her. 'What you need is a good strong coffee,' she said sympathetically, taking Lucinda's arm. 'Come with me.'

In the kitchen, Rachel uttered a silent prayer of thanks that she'd watched Orlando fill the kettle earlier and knew how to do it.

'Thanks,' said Lucinda gratefully, taking the mug of coffee. 'You don't know how much I needed this. You're a lifesaver.'

Rachel smiled. 'My pleasure.' It was true. It was a pleasure to be doing something useful for once. 'Just tell me what else I can do to help.'

'Oh, don't say that or I might just take you up on it,' groaned Lucinda, reaching into the depths of her bag and pulling out some paracetamol. 'I feel rotten.'

'Oh, you poor thing.' Rachel regarded her sympathetically over the rim of her mug. 'Are you coming down with the flu, do you think?'

'Let's hope not. Or, if I am, let's hope I can keep it at bay until this party's in full swing.' Lucinda suddenly looked a lot less confident, and Rachel could see that much of the glossy sophistication was just a veneer. 'The thing is,' she went on miserably, 'the business is in a spot of bother, and this party could be make or break. I can't afford to mess this up—it's the perfect opportunity to get some new clients from amongst all these loaded financiers. That's why I was banking on the capable Mrs Harper.'

'I'm afraid I'm hardly capable, but I'll do whatever I can to help,' said Rachel apologetically.

Lucinda looked relieved. 'Would you? I don't suppose you could find a solution to the flower crisis, could you?'

Outside it had stopped snowing, but the temperature had dropped. Rachel's feet, in borrowed Wellingtons, hugely too big for her, crunched through a crisp crust of perfect snow as she trudged along an avenue flanked on both side by sculptural pleached limes.

There was something incredibly beautiful about their bare branches against the frozen sky, something poignant about the way their natural forms had been trained into rigidly controlled shape. They reminded her of Orlando, the way he'd appeared in the kitchen last night. Caged. Restrained.

Her arms were full of branches—some bare, some adorned with berries, some still covered in leaves the same coppery colour as her hair—her hands were scratched and torn, but she didn't care, and her cheeks were flushed with cautious triumph. Following the lime avenue to its end, she'd discovered a gate in the wall and, with difficulty, pushed it open, hoping to find neat borders of well-behaved shrubs. Instead she had found a tangled wilderness.

She'd almost turned back, but the thought of letting Lucinda down, of failing, had made her persevere. She was glad she had. Ahead of her now, Easton Hall was a picture of English perfection, its ancient brick rosy against the stark, snow covered landscape. It was so beautiful, but there was something sad and empty about it—as if it knew that the best days, the happy times, were gone and there was only darkness ahead. Rachel wondered about all the previous generations of Wintertons who had lived and laughed and loved here; thought of family Christmases and summer afternoons with tea on the lawn, of parties like the one tonight in former years, when all the family would have been gathered…

Now there was just Orlando.

Her heart gave a painful twist inside her chest, as if it had been impaled on one of the thorny branches she carried. He seemed so isolated. She longed to draw him, and this magical house, back into warmth and light.

But of course, she thought sadly, dodging past the caterer's vans and pushing open the front door with her hip, if anyone was to warm Orlando's chilly heart or bring the smile back to his beautiful, hard face it wouldn't be her.

It would be this Arabella.

She paused, struggling to keep hold of all the damp, tangled branches as she kicked off the ridiculous boots. But, though they were far too big for her, they stubbornly refused to come off, so that she was reduced to hopping madly on one foot, desperately shaking her leg in the air while trying not to fall over.

At last the boot flew from her foot and skidded across the tiled floor, coming to rest at the feet of the person standing there. The person she hadn't noticed. The person who had just watched her stupid, ungainly embarrassing display and not stepped in to help.

Orlando.

'My God,' he said, in a cool, mocking voice. 'Burnham Wood comes to Dunsinane. The question is, *why*? We have plenty of kindling and firewood in the kitchen yard.'

Scarlet with exertion and embarrassment, Rachel eyed him mutinously through her armful of spiky branches.

'These are flowers for the tables,' she said haughtily.

Orlando's finely arched eyebrows shot up, eloquently communicating his scorn.

'Really?'

Rachel dropped her gaze. How could anyone manage to get so many syllables out of such a short word? Pig. No wonder he was alone. It was because he was insufferable.

She hesitated for a moment, horribly aware of her mad hair and unmade-up face. Her nose was probably bright red from the cold, and she desperately wanted to blow it. She sniffed, loudly.

'Yes, really. Now, if you'll excuse me…' She took a step forward, intending to sweep past him in an attitude of preoccupation and importance, but she'd forgotten she was still wearing one Wellington, which gave her a madly lopsided gait. She stopped, fury and humiliation warring within her as she had no alternative but to try to lever it off with her other foot.

Orlando took a step towards her, his face perfectly impassive. 'Can I help?'

It was too much. Desperate to end this humiliating encounter, and get as far away from him as possible, Rachel gave an almighty lunge to try and free her foot. Unfortunately as she did so she failed to step clear of the top of the boot and, unable to put her arms out, overbalanced.

He caught her effortlessly and set her back on her feet again. And then he stood back, snatching his hands away as if, instead of being chilled from the frozen garden, she'd been blistering hot.

'Thanks,' Rachel muttered stiffly, and, gathering the branches closer to her, resumed her progress across the hall, choking on the bitterness of the irony.

She had, after all, been the one to bring a smile back to Orlando Winterton's face. Such a damned shame, she reflected savagely, that it had been one of such complete and utter contempt.

The light was beginning to fade as Rachel finished the last of the arrangements and placed it on the table in the hallway.

Lucinda had brought heavy rectangular glass vases, tall

enough to support the height of the branches. They rose starkly out of the glass, and against the opulent grandeur of Easton Hall looked astonishingly sparse and elegant.

Rachel stood back and allowed herself a small moment of satisfaction.

She had tried something new, and she hadn't failed dismally. With a spring in her step, she went to find Lucinda.

She was in the dining room, talking to one of the hordes of caterers who had been traipsing in and out all day, carrying vast platters of salmon and lobster, endless dishes of salad, and every kind of spectacular pudding imaginable. But, going into the room, Rachel felt her attention drawn away from the array of food laid out on the long tables by the rising hysteria in Lucinda's voice.

'I quite specifically asked you to supply the candles. It's no good telling me now that you haven't got them!'

'I'm sorry.' The caterer's tone was firm. 'That wasn't the message we got. I double-checked myself this morning what we we'd been commissioned to supply, and candles weren't on the list.'

'So you're trying to tell me—?'

Rachel laid a hand on Lucinda's arm. She could feel her shivering violently.

'Don't worry. I'll go out and get some. The table arrangements are all done, so I've got nothing else to do.'

Lucinda turned to face her. She was deathly pale, but spots of bright colour burned high up on her cheeks.

'Would you?' Her eyes filled with tears. 'That would be fantastic.'

Rachel drew her away from the caterer, lowering her voice. 'Lucinda, you look dreadful.'

'I feel dreadful,' she said through chattering teeth. Two fat tears slid down her cheeks. 'I don't know what to do.'

'Go to bed,' said Rachel resolutely. 'You have to. You're obviously awfully unwell.'

'But I can't!' There's still so much to do!'

'Doesn't matter.' Rachel put her arm around her. Lucinda was burning hot and, crying in earnest now, virtually unrecognisable from the sleek, capable-looking girl who had so intimidated Rachel earlier. 'The caterers can sort out the drinks, and I'm going to buy candles right now. But you can't drive back to London like this.'

'No, I know…' She sighed, looking up at Rachel with puffy eyes. 'My godmother lives about ten miles from here, just beyond the next village. I'm sure she'd put me up.'

'Phone her,' ordered Rachel. 'I'll drop you off on my way into town.'

'Hadn't you better check with Lord Ashbroke?'

Rachel was about to say yes, but then she remembered the contemptuous look he had given her earlier, and his attitude of terrifying remoteness. 'I'm sure he's far too busy to be disturbed.'

'You're wonderful,' said Lucinda gratefully, giving her a weak hug.

Rachel smiled sadly.

That, unfortunately, was a matter of opinion.

CHAPTER SEVEN

THE snow had transformed the lanes along which she had hurtled so desperately only the day before. The black, glowering landscape was now hidden in a soft white blanket, which sparkled in the beam of her headlamps as if it had been sprinkled with glitter in preparation for tonight's party.

Driving carefully back to Easton, Rachel raised her hand, tentatively brushing it up the back of her neck.

She felt strange; oddly light-headed, and the sensation of the close-cropped hair at her nape brought an involuntary smile to her face in the warm fug of the car. She had gone into the hairdresser's completely on impulse as she'd hurried by on her search for candles, and had found herself seated in front of the mirror before she'd had time to think about what she was doing.

The face that had looked back at her had been pale and childlike. Her eyes had always been her best feature—large, as clear and warm as amber, and inherited from her father, her mother had once told her in disgust—but they gave her face a frightened look.

And as she'd sat there the words she had said to Orlando last night came back to her. *I'm tired of being afraid. I want to be brave...*

She'd taken a deep breath and heard herself saying 'Take it all off, please.'

Now, she glanced into the driving mirror, angling her head for a better view of herself. The hairdresser, horrified at the sacrilege of butchering such luxuriant hair, had flatly refused to give her a short crop, persuading her instead into the idea of a choppy, layered bob, cut closely into the curve of her skull at the back and angling sharply downwards, following the line of her jaw to finish in longer, spiky layers at the front.

It felt glorious. She slid her hand into the front, pushing it backwards, loving the way it stayed put now the weight of it had gone.

Only now did she appreciate what a weight it had been. Described by the PR people as being 'integral to the brand', her heavy hair had been entangled with the weight of expectation and responsibility. It had oppressed her and, while defining her image, it had stopped her from being herself.

She was free of all that now—in every way. It was as if Orlando Winterton had broken all the chains that had anchored her to her past with the same casual ruthlessness with which he and his fellow pilots torched pianos.

It was only natural that she should feel drawn to him, she thought sadly. It was inevitable, stemming from the same psychological imperative that made newly hatched ducklings bond with the first creature they saw when they emerged from the egg. He was the first person who had listened to her, the first person she felt had ever really *seen* her—seen through the image and past her porcelain-pretty face.

It was just such a damned shame he was in love with someone else. Suddenly she gave a gasp as the road ahead narrowed. She slammed her foot on the brakes, but too late, too sharply, and she felt the car glide across the icy road, completely out of her control. For a moment everything was suspended as in slow motion she watched the low wall ahead getting closer, brighter in the beam of the headlights…

And then there was a crunch, a jolt, a shattering of glass, and semi-darkness as the headlight on one side went out.

In the sudden thick silence Rachel let out a shaky laugh.

That bloody bridge again.

Which just went to show that knowing where the dangers lay didn't stop you falling right into them.

The house was completely quiet as she pushed open the front door and stood for a moment in the hallway with her bags of shopping. Cold, intimidating, dark—just as it had been when she'd stood here for the first time yesterday, almost deranged with terror.

The team of caterers must have finished here and be getting themselves organised in the kitchen. Apart from a glimpse of long, white-clothed tables through the open door of the dining room beyond the hallway, there was no evidence at all that in a little under two hours this would be the scene of a party.

For a moment Rachel felt an icy fist of doubt bunch inside her stomach. *She* had been the one who had insisted Lucinda went home, so the responsibility for making things happen now rested firmly on her shoulders.

How had Lucinda put it?

Oh, knickers.

She set the supermarket bags down and looked inside them. Having her hair cut had taken up more time than she'd thought, and by the time she'd left the hairdressers all the small shops on the high street had been shut. Suppressing her panic, she'd re-membered passing a huge supermarket on the way in, and there she had found boxes of thick ivory-coloured church candles and filled her basket with as many as she could carry.

Hurrying to the checkout, she had spotted, on a shelf of reduced post-Christmas stock, some fairy lights. Shaped like snowflakes, they'd reminded her of watching the snow fall last night, standing naked at the window of the firelit drawing room, with Orlando at her side...

For a second she had seen, more vividly than the boxes on the shelves in front of her, his deep-set, slanting eyes. Pale green, ringed with darkness. Tropical waters overlaid with ice.

It had come as a surprise to discover, as she'd paid for her shopping at the checkout, that as well as the candles she also seemed to have bought five boxes of the snowflake-shaped fairy lights.

Now, with trembling hands, she set to work.

Orlando stood in front of the mirror.

If he looked straight ahead, straight to where his face should be, technically he should just about be able to bring into the lower edge of his vision the buttonholes down the front of his dress shirt. But for the thousandth time the tiny mother-of-pearl shirt stud slipped from his fingers and fell to the floor.

He swore expressively, and was just about to get down and try to locate the stud with his hands when there was a soft knock on the door.

'Yes?'

God, he sounded like an ogre. He felt like a bloody ogre. He was losing his humanity along with his sight. Wrestling with self-loathing, he deliberately didn't turn his head as he heard the door open.

'Orlando?'

That voice. Soft. Like the cashmere she wore. But with a slight edge...a texture too...like...

'What?'

'I'm so sorry to disturb you.' She was crossing the room. In the mirror he caught a glimpse of movement behind him, a glimmer of her brilliant hair. 'I can't fasten this dress. I wondered if you could possibly do it?'

That again. He turned round slowly to face her. 'How does it fasten?' he said dully, holding up his bandaged fingers. 'Because I'm struggling too.'

'Zip. You should manage with one hand. And then I'll help you.'

He felt the usual, automatic kick of bone-deep, visceral resentment at the word, but gritted his teeth and said, 'Fine. Turn round.'

Did he imagine the small, sad sigh as she presented her back to him?

Instinctively he reached up with his injured hand to sweep the hair from her neck, but found nothing there. Of course—she must have fastened it up. Imagined visions of her bare nape rose tormentingly in his mind, but determinedly he kept his head lowered, his gaze fixed straight ahead, deliberately not trying to get it within his field of vision. His fingers sought the base of the zip.

It began low down, in the small of her back. His fingers skimmed across the luxuriously soft fabric to where it met the satin warmth of her skin and he almost snatched his hand away.

'Can you manage?'

That was what her voice reminded him of, he thought, brushing his thumb downwards, smoothing her dress. Velvet. Dark, luxurious, sexy velvet.

'Of course,' he snapped, tugging the zip upwards. 'Done.'

'Thank you.' She turned to face him again. 'Now you.'

Downstairs, the house was finally ready, and she hoped it was almost up to Lucinda's standard. But the time had sped by, and she had left barely half an hour to wreak the same magic on herself as she had on the vast, chilly rooms. Rushing upstairs, she had showered in record time and, with shaking hands, had brushed the lightest smudge of charcoal-grey glittering shadow over her eyelids, adding a slick of shimmering gloss to lips that already felt swollen and red. Finally she had slipped into the dress she was to have worn at her big recital in Paris, at the end of her honeymoon. A narrow, figure hugging column of dark green crushed velvet, it had come to no harm from being squashed into her suitcase for two days.

For five long minutes she'd struggled with the zip, before giving in and coming to find him. But from the moment she'd walked in here and seen him, his shirt open to the waist, the long cuffs hanging down over his beautiful hands, she had felt sick with desire. And now this was almost more than she could bear.

It was like some sophisticated form of torture. Picking up one of the antique shirt studs, Rachel tried to slot it into the lowest buttonhole, just above the place where his stomach swept down in a muscular arc beneath his ribs. Only centimetres from his bare skin, her hand trembled violently with the need to touch it. She gripped the stud between her fingers, focusing intently on the gold-hinged stem and waiting for the dizzying wave of longing to pass before she could fit it through the hole.

It was so stupid, so very, very stupid, to feel like this when he belonged to someone else. There was no point going back over what had happened last night—that had been before she'd known about Arabella, and had come with no promises, only pure, heat-of-the-moment passion…

She shuddered, biting back a moan as the stud slipped through her fingers.

'Sorry—I don't know what's wrong with me.'

She dropped to her knees and swept a hand over the rough sisal floor covering, groping for the stud. Suddenly the symbolism of her position struck her—she was literally on the floor at his feet. She had to get a grip of herself. Standing up, she took a deep breath.

'Sorry. Try again.'

He had promised her nothing. She slid the stud into place and reached for another. *He had given her no reason to think he had any feelings for her whatsoever.* Another stud. *He hadn't even seemed to notice her hair.* What had she expected? That he'd take one look at her and decide Arabella wasn't the one for him after all? God, how ridiculous. Angrily, she picked up another stud.

And made the mistake of glancing up at him.

He was staring straight past her, over her head, his clear green eyes empty and bleak, his jaw tense, as if he was enduring some terrible private torment. She looked quickly away, sliding the stud into the buttonhole in the middle of his chest. Over his heart.

Arabella. He was wishing she was Arabella.

Misery fought with compassion. In that brief moment when she'd looked at him she had seen on his face an expression that exactly mirrored her own feelings. The difference was that she had the ability to ease his suffering a little. Arabella had told her not to say anything, but would it be so wrong to comfort him with the news that she was coming back?

He lifted his chin so she could put the last stud into the collar of his shirt, revealing the strong column of his throat. For a second she couldn't move, mesmerised by the pulse that jumped faintly beneath the smooth skin. In an instant all thoughts of Arabella fled her mind—along with everything else but the desperate urge to press her lips against it. Aware that her own heart was beating in perfect time, she almost bit through her lip in anguish as she snapped the stud into place and immediately backed away.

'Thanks.' His tone was utterly offhand.

She swallowed. If he had noticed her lack of composure, he was doing a very good job of not showing it. Probably because it embarrassed the hell out of him.

Or maybe he just didn't notice her at all.

'No problem. If that's all, I'll go…'

Gathering up a handful of floor-skimming green crushed velvet, she almost ran to the door, choking back the ridiculous urge to cry. The dress, the haircut, the eyeshadow and lipgloss had been wasted. He hadn't even glanced twice at her.

She couldn't get away fast enough, Orlando thought bitterly. He had sensed her awkwardness, and from it could deduce only one thing.

His suspicions were correct.

Arabella had told her.

Blackness flooded his heart as he turned to her with an icy smile. Let her squirm with embarrassment at his helplessness. Let her see exactly how big a mistake she'd made last night.

'Sorry,' he drawled, in a voice of molten steel. 'I'm afraid you'll have to do the cufflinks too.'

She hesitated, then came slowly back towards him. He could see that her hair half covered her face, giving him the agonising impression that she'd just stumbled out of bed—sleepy and tousled. As she bent her head over his outstretched hands he felt one silken strand brush the inside of his wrist.

Fire licked through him, searing his scarred emotions with fresh agony.

Her long, strong fingers worked quickly at the stiff cuffs of his shirt, folding them back, slipping the flat disc of century-old gold with its worn Ashbroke crest through the holes. He could hear her breathing, fast and shallow, smell the scent of crushed rose petals, with its whispers of summer and happiness, its memories of last night.

All things that he had lost for ever.

She straightened up and rubbed the palms of her hands down the narrow column of her fitted dress. Against the dark velvet the skin of her bare shoulders gleamed like mother-of-pearl.

'I can manage the rest,' he snarled, turning away.

'You're sure? Your tie?'

'I've done it often enough.'

'With one hand?' There was a break in her voice that sounded like anguish. Or pity.

He swung round and felt his fists clench, the throbbing in his fingers reminding him afresh of the ostensible reason for needing her help. Picking up the silk bow tie, he hesitated for a moment as his mind filled with dense, dark fog. Then, trying to keep the hostility from his face, he turned back to her and tossed the tie at her.

'No.'

She caught it, and for a second just stood—not daring to look at him, unable to bear his obvious distaste at having her so close. She threaded the band of silk through her fingers, twisting and pleating the expensive material, numbly watching as a tear fell onto it and slowly melted into the darkness.

'Do I have to beg?'

The ice in his tone made her gasp. Her head jerked up, and she gazed at him through a haze of humiliated tears. He gazed back, his green eyes glittering with cruelty.

'I'm sorry.'

Even in high heels, she had to stand on tiptoe to slip the tie around his neck. The proximity was almost unbearable. Staring fixedly at his lean jaw, she made a clumsy attempt to tie a neat, flat bow, but the pounding blood in her ears and the echoing drumbeat in her wrists, her heart, the top of her thighs, made her fingers flutter ineffectually at the heavy silk. She could feel the whisper of his breath fanning her brow and heard her own whimper of anguish.

'I can't—'

He swore abruptly as his hands closed over hers. His face was like granite. She was aware of nothing beyond his skin on hers as he wrenched her hands from him. 'Leave it. I'll do it.'

'How can you?' she cried, disgusted at her own inadequacy, her own emotional stupidity. 'I can do it—please, just let me try again…'

And then his hands were on her face, holding it, his thumbs brushing her cheeks as the tears soaked into the bandage on his fingers before he pulled away sharply and thrust his hands through his dark, dishevelled hair. He half turned from her, but she heard his exasperated sigh and felt herself die inside a little more. 'You're crying. Why?'

'Nothing. I'm being stupid. Take no notice…' She gave a sudden, bitter laugh. 'Not that you would anyway…'

He whipped back to face her. His eyes blazed with sudden searing, unidentifiable passion, but his voice was terrifyingly calm.

'What did Arabella say, exactly?'

Rachel felt her hands fly to her mouth. 'She…she told me not to tell you.'

Orlando went very still. Standing there with his head thrown back, the silk tie hanging loosely around his neck, he looked like a tortured Adonis, and she felt the breath being squeezed from her lungs by the sheer charisma of his presence as she waited for him to speak.

'I can guess.' He gave her a heart breaking twisted smile, and his tone softened so that the steel edge to it was almost imperceptible. Which only made it more dangerous. 'Discretion was never really Arabella's strong point.'

Rachel was like a rabbit caught in the headlights of a fast-approaching car. His face was completely expressionless, utterly remote, but the emotion that flared in his luminous eyes was terrifying.

'I think it's best that I…know…' She was backing away from him, unable to bear his nearness and his immeasurable distance a moment longer. 'I was in danger…in very great danger—' her voice broke into a dry sob '—of falling in love with you, you see.'

She stumbled slightly on the hem of her trailing dress, and then, yanking it up over her knees, turned and fled from the room.

CHAPTER EIGHT

STANDING in the hallway beneath the portrait of his great grandfather, Orlando drained one glass of champagne and picked up another.

The house was filling up. The level of noise rose as more parties of people arrived, greeting each other loudly, their confident voices ringing through Easton's vast rooms and all but drowning out the sound of Lucinda's string quartet. The ball showed every sign of being a huge success, and the weather, far from deterring people from coming, seemed to have forged a sort of Dunkirk spirit amongst the guests. In their midst, Orlando felt more isolated than ever.

It wasn't his damaged sight that set him apart from everyone else, though. It was his relentless, churning rage.

At Arabella. She'd probably told half of London that Orlando the heroic was now Orlando the pitiful. But he'd been a fool to expect anything else; she'd always been as hard as diamonds. It was what had first attracted him to her.

No. It was Rachel who had hurt him the most.

'I think it's best that I know—I was in danger of falling in love with you...'

Was.

Not now. Not now she'd found out the truth about him.

There was a blast of arctic air as another group came in, pausing to hand over tickets and coats to the door staff, cheerfully exchanging anecdotes about their difficult journeys as they helped themselves to champagne from the tray. Orlando knew that he should be there, playing the host, but even thinking about the effort required made him feel weary. Turning on his heel, he walked in the other direction—towards the inner hall, away from the throng of people.

The house looked stunning. Even through the acrid fog of his anger and the curse of his reduced sight, he could feel that Easton been brought to life. He had been so used to its shadows and darkness that he had quite simply forgotten that it could be so lovely. He ought to find Lucinda and thank her…

He felt his mouth quirk into a twisted smile.

But he'd have to recognise her first. He'd known her for years, but still his chances of being able to pick her out from all the other pedigree blondes at the party were utterly negligible.

Despairingly he shouldered his way through the groups of people who were clustered, talking in loud, braying voices, in the hallway at the foot of the stairs. He had just reached the door to the dining room when he stopped, his fingers tightening dangerously around his glass as he overheard two men behind him.

'Check that out. Coming down the stairs…'

The second man let out a low whistle. 'Hel-lo. Don't usually go for redheads, but for her I'd make an exception. Look at the t—'

Orlando stopped dead, adrenaline coursing through him. Technically, he was the host of this party. Did that make knocking one of the guests unconscious more acceptable, or less?

'I say, isn't it that girl from the posters? The pianist one? Hair's different, but I'd recognise her anywhere. Huge picture of her at Bank tube station last year. Used to make my journey to work quite uncomfortable, I can *tell* you…'

As they burst into guffaws of crude laughter, Orlando wrenched open the door into the courtyard and stepped out into the biting cold, feeling a small flicker of satisfaction as he heard one of them say, 'Bloody hell, it's freezing!'

He was shaking, so fired up with bitterness and adrenaline that it took him a moment to take in his surroundings.

The high-walled courtyard, where light hardly penetrated for most of the year, was bathed in the gentle glow of scores of candles. They lined the snowy paths, were clustered in flickering groups on the steps opposite and in each corner of the courtyard, and reflected a hundredfold in the rows of windows that looked out onto it.

His footsteps slowed as he reached the point in the centre where the paths converged and turned slowly round, exhaling heavily in a plume of frozen air.

Lucinda had done a great job, he realised with a small frisson of surprise. In truth, he'd only hired her because he'd known her vaguely from the old days and had heard her business was in trouble. But she was good. Amazingly good. The effect she'd created out here and in the house with firelight and candles was magical. Timeless, somehow, as if somehow the years had been peeled back and the house was in its heyday again.

He took one of the paths that crossed the courtyard and stood in the shadows against the wall, eyes closed, waiting for the unexpected tightening in his throat to ease.

The volume of voices and laughter suddenly grew louder for a moment, and then died down again, but the faint strains of the string quartet drifted through the frozen air, like warm, caressing fingers.

'Orlando?'

Rachel laid a hand on his arm and felt him stiffen instantly. His eyes flew open and, gazing up, she could see the candlelight reflected in their cold, glittering depths.

'I came to find you. I wanted to apologise…'

He cut her off ruthlessly with a swift, crushing sneer. 'There's nothing to *apologise* for. At least you were honest.'

'But I shouldn't have been. It was wrong of me to say that about…about falling in love with you when—'

'Save it,' he spat. He made to move past her, but she grabbed his arm, her strong pianist's fingers gripping him. He froze, holding up his arm where she held him, too bound by ingrained chivalry to shake her off, almost afraid of what might happen if he unleashed the fury that surged through him at that moment. Around him, the candles still flickered serenely, mocking him, taunting him with the memory of his momentary glimpse of a peace that would forever elude him.

'Let go of me, Rachel.'

'No! Please, Orlando, I want to explain—about Arabella. I didn't have a chance to finish before, to tell you that she—'

'I don't want to hear it!' he roared. His fingers closed around her wrist like handcuffs and brutally he wrenched her hand off him. But somehow his grip remained locked fast on her wrist and they struggled, her other hand coming up to his chest, pushing him away, beating against him, until neither of them was sure who was struggling against whom. With a desperate cry Rachel tried to break away, only to find he was still holding her, pulling her back towards him, into his body, and she fell against him, so that he had to grasp her waist to stop her falling.

And then suddenly his hands were on her back, and her lips were parting as his mouth came down on hers, and her fingers were entangled in his hair, pulling, pressing his head down harder, wanting more, wanting all of him. There was no tenderness in the kiss, just an urgency born of despair and frustration and pain and longing. She could feel the wall behind her, cold and damp, but she was glad of its solidity as she leaned back against it, unable to trust her legs to hold her up. Orlando's hands were on her shoulders now, pressing them back against the brick—or was she doing that herself?—her body helplessly arching towards him in an attitude of transparent need. She could feel her legs part, her hips rising upwards as his hand slipped downwards. His grip was hard, insistent, and it sent her to the brink of oblivion.

So what if he loved Arabella? *So what?* He was here, with her; this was real—the only reality she could think of. The world beyond this tiny space of shared breath, shared warmth, shared fire, was crushed out of her consciousness by his presence and his nearness and her own self-destructive will.

She needed him.

Now.

She needed him now, and if she didn't have him she thought she would die.

She heard him groan, his lips pressed against her neck, as his hand slid upwards into her hair, feeling the spiky shortness at her nape. She felt the sudden rush of chill air on her heated skin as he drew his head back and, opening her eyes, saw him gazing down at her with a despairing intensity that sent a wave of annihilating desire crashing through her, drenching her from the inside.

'Your hair…'

She didn't let him get any further. Taking his face in both her hands, she pulled him roughly down again. For a moment she let her quivering lips hover tormentingly over his, until she heard his tiny indrawn breath and knew he was as lost as she was. The moment stretched, deepened, as she slowly slid her tongue along the taut line of his top lip…

'Good Lord….' A woman's voice cut through the raw air, almost as cold and sharp as the icicles hanging from the eaves above them. 'I thought it was a country ball, not an orgy.'

Rachel felt Orlando stiffen and jerk upright, heard his low, savage curse.

She recognised the voice from the phone call that morning, but now it was stripped of its veneer of concern, revealing the viciousness beneath. Her eyes flew to the doorway. Silhouetted against the bright hallway beyond, her face illuminated by the candles into a grotesque mask of malice, stood a woman with long blonde hair.

'Arabella.'

With lightning speed Orlando moved so that he was standing between them, shielding Rachel with his body from the basilisk stare of the blonde.

'I told you I was coming,' she drawled. 'You should know me well enough to know that when I say something I mean it. I suppose I should consider myself lucky to have arrived in the middle of a party, when there was someone to show me in, since you're obviously far too preoccupied.' She tossed her blonde mane disdainfully. 'I left my things in the study and helped myself to a drink—you don't mind, do you?'

'Yes. I told you to stay away.'

'You did, didn't you?'

Slumped, shivering, against the wall, Rachel could hear the spiteful relish in her tone. She's enjoying this, she thought dully. Her moment of victory as she returns to lay claim to her man. She could picture the triumph on that tight, hard face, but could see nothing but the broad spread of Orlando's shoulders. She pressed her hands against the bricks to stop herself from reaching out and sliding her arms around him, desperate for the warmth and strength of him, but suddenly realised why he had positioned himself like that. Not to protect her from Arabella, but to hide her.

He was ashamed.

'But,' Arabella continued, 'unfortunately, darling, you Wintertons aren't the gods you once thought you were. You don't command the universe any more, and things happen whether you like it or not.'

He had taken a step forward as she spoke. Behind him, Rachel could sense his tension in the set of his shoulders, the proud tilt of his head. She closed her eyes, wishing she didn't have to endure the torture of seeing him go to her.

'What do you want, Arabella?'

'I have something to show you,' Arabella said matter-of-factly. 'Oh, dear—maybe that's not a very tactful way of putting it. Sorry, darling. But you'll forgive me when you find out what it is. It's in the library…' And with that she disappeared back into the noise and warmth of the party.

For a moment Orlando didn't move. Standing there, in the centre of the candlelit courtyard, he suddenly reminded Rachel of some early martyr, alone and palpably suffering. Slowly he turned his head. The candles cast deep shadows in the hollows of his face, making him look gaunt and haunted.

'Go,' Rachel croaked. 'Go. This is what she told me on the phone. What she asked me not to tell you. This is what I was trying to explain…'

He shook his head, frowning.

'What? *What*?'

'She told me that she was coming down here…coming to see you. She wants you back, Orlando. She told me not to tell you.'

'God, Rachel…I got it wrong. I thought…' His head dipped and he thrust his hands into his hair, then took a couple of steps towards her. She held up her hands.

'Doesn't matter. Please. I'm fine. Just go to her.'

She said the words. But she couldn't bear to watch him as he walked away.

'Sorry to drag you away from your guests,' drawled Arabella bitchily as she stood at Orlando's desk in the library. 'Not that you were doing much in the way of socialising. I must say I'm stunned to find you haven't lost that Winterton magic, Orlando darling. I'm delighted to see you're as attractive and commanding as ever.'

'Are you? I see no reason at all why you should care, as there's absolutely nothing between us any more.'

Arabella gave a dry, humourless laugh. 'Oh, darling, you don't know how devastatingly ironic that remark is.'

She paused, and he saw her walk around to the other side of the desk and bend to pick something up. He tilted his head back, trying to see what it was. Something large and cumbersome. He heard the heavy thud as she placed it on the desk, but couldn't make sense of the awkward shape.

'There. *There*, darling, is the reason why I care. Do you see it now?'

Her tone was spiteful. Orlando felt hatred harden into chips of ice in his heart.

'No, Arabella, I don't see,' he said in a low, savage tone. 'As you very well know.'

'I don't *know*, actually. I know what the doctors said, of course, and I thought by now you'd be helpless—an invalid.' She sounded aggrieved, as if she were almost disappointed to be proved wrong. 'But you seem completely normal—as that little nobody out there would obviously agree. I take it she doesn't know?'

'That's none of your business.'

'It's rather obvious from the way that she looked at you that she doesn't—like you're Prince Charming and Sir Lancelot all rolled into one. I'd keep it that way, if I were you—telling her that her hero is flawed would be like telling a child that Father Christmas doesn't exist.'

Orlando spun round, feeling for the door handle, knowing that if he stayed in the same room as her no amount of chivalry, training or good breeding would prevent him from giving vent to the violent impulses that fizzed and burned like overloaded electrical circuits through his nerve-endings. He wanted to get back to Rachel, but he paused for a moment and said, with quiet venom, 'I don't know why you came back, Arabella, but you needn't have bothered. There's nothing you can say that would—'

Orlando stopped dead as a thin, quavering cry rang out into the tense air from the direction of the desk. His hand froze on the door handle as his blood froze in his veins.

'Nothing?' challenged Arabella in the silence that followed. Her voice vibrated with unconcealed triumph. 'How about *come and meet your son*?'

Back in the hallway, the light and noise of the party were like an assault after the tranquil courtyard. Rachel looked around in bewilderment. Her lips were swollen with Orlando's kisses, her hair mussed from his questing, hungry fingers, and a combination of surging hormones and desperate longing made her feel edgy and wild. Thrusting her way through the crowd, she ignored the comments and whistles of the financiers and hedge fund boys in her wake, and made her way resolutely to the library.

She had to find out what was going on.

Her heels tapped on the marble tiles of the hallway as she approached the half-open door. She could see Orlando standing there, his hand on the handle, but then she felt her confident footsteps falter as she heard Arabella's voice…

'*Come and meet your son…*'

Rachel stopped dead. Through a crack in the door she saw Arabella's face. She bore the look of a chess grandmaster who had just uttered the word *checkmate*.

On the desk, from the depths of a bulky infant carrier seat, Rachel caught a fleeting glimpse of a tiny flailing hand before Orlando slammed the door shut, leaving her shivering on the outside.

'Is it mine?'

Arabella made a sharp, scornful exclamation. 'If you could see him you wouldn't be asking. He's Winterton through and through—from the top of his very dark head to the tips of his long, elegant fingers,' she sneered. 'If he wasn't I wouldn't be in the mess I am now.'

Orlando walked slowly over to the window, trying to keep as much distance between himself and Arabella. And this child. His head felt as if it was full of sand, and he rubbed his forehead with his undamaged hand, trying to clear it. Trying to rub away the images of Rachel that wouldn't seem to leave him.

'What mess?'

'Jamie's kicked me out,' she said dully. 'I thought the baby was his, but, given that Jamie is deliciously Scandinavian and blond, it's painfully bloody obvious that it isn't.'

'You must have known that from the dates?' Orlando ground out from between gritted teeth. Arabella left nothing to chance. Her body ran to the same strictly controlled timetable as the rest of her life.

He heard her sigh. 'It must have happened that last couple of weeks. When you were…told. Diagnosed. Whatever. Felix was home…' For a moment her voice faltered, and then hardened, almost defensively. 'It was a horrible time for me. I was so confused. I didn't have anyone to talk to…'

Orlando's face was a mask of contempt, and it dripped from every sneering word. 'Poor you.'

'It was hell! You never talked to me. You just pushed me away!'

'Funny,' said Orlando acidly. 'That isn't how I remember it. As I recall, you ran out of the room when I told you what Parkes had said, and went back to London that afternoon for some party.' He swore softly. 'Oh, God. What a coincidence. Jamie van Hartesvelt's party…'

'I was shocked…devastated—surely you can understand that! I needed space to think—to adjust,' Arabella protested. 'Suddenly you weren't the same person any more, the man I'd fallen in love with. And then, when I came back the next day, you hardly acknowledged my existence. If it hadn't been for Felix I don't know how I would have coped…' She was silent for a moment, and then added, almost in an undertone, 'Felix was good to me.'

'Of course he was,' said Orlando bitterly. 'Because he'd won. Everything we ever did was in competition with each other, and suddenly it was over. I was out. Defeated. He was the winner, so he could afford to be bloody *good* to you.'

'It wasn't like that! He was devastated too. He looked up to you so much, Orlando, and the thought of you being…weakened, being *reduced*, was almost more than he could bear! I wasn't surprised when I heard that he was dead. He shouldn't have been flying. He was still too upset.'

'Oh, for God's sake, spare me the guilt trip! I'm supposed to believe now that Felix's death is due to my selfish, embarrassing *weakness*? Jeez, Arabella—does it not enter your stupid, self-absorbed head that it's bad enough knowing that I'm here, sentenced to this bloody awful half-life, while Felix has been robbed of a useful, long, full one? Don't you think that's bad enough without you telling me it's actually *my fault*? Don't you think I'd change places with him without a second's hesitation? The only thing that makes it bearable is the knowledge that wherever he is now, he's laughing because he won. From here to eternity he's a *hero*, for God's sake!'

She raised her head, and it was lucky that Orlando couldn't see the look of cruel triumph on her face. 'Oh, yes,' she said quietly. 'That destroys you, doesn't it, Orlando? Felix died a hero, while you're living the life of a hermit.'

Above the drumming of blood in his ears, Orlando heard the sound of Arabella unbuckling the straps of the baby seat, and the soft sigh and whimper of the child as she picked him up. 'It's a bit of a come-down, isn't it, darling, after the accolades and the adulation? Just as well Felix did his bit to uphold the family name. Just as well he's a good role model for your son. That's why I called him after his brave uncle. Meet Felix.'

Orlando felt the blood drain from his face. The room was very still, very quiet. The sounds of the party were coming to them as if from a parallel universe, not merely from the other side of a closed door. Eventually Orlando spoke. His voice was hollow.

'Why? Why did you do that?'

'Because I did everything to make you love me,' Arabella hissed venomously. 'I was *perfect*. You have no idea how much effort it took to be perfect all the time, and it still wasn't enough. You didn't love me. You didn't need me. You had everything and I was just an accessory. But in all that time we were together I came to understand you, and I knew the one person who could really touch your impenetrable heart was Felix. You loved him, but you hated him, too.'

He had to hand it to her. Her aim had been to inflict the maximum amount of pain and she had succeeded. She was right, and he'd underestimated her. She'd made sure in the most subtle, agonising way possible that he would never be allowed to forget Felix's victory. Felix's heroism. His own fallibility.

'Well done,' he said bleakly. 'It seems you've won too. What now?'

'I haven't bloody well won. I'm the loser in all this, Orlando. It's destroyed my life, my career, my relationship, my *body*, for God's sake.' She was pacing briskly back and forth across the room, bouncing the inert bundle in her arms with alarming ferocity. 'It's harder than it looks, this parenting thing. No sleep. No going out. No time do have a bath or talk on the phone or go shopping. It's suffocating. Everybody's always on at me not to drink and smoke—as if I hadn't already given up enough.'

Orlando felt the sweat break out on the back of his neck as this insight into the early weeks of his child's life was starkly revealed. He stepped forward, his hands in his pockets so she couldn't see his clenched fists, but she was too wrapped up in herself to notice anything else.

Her voice had taken on a slightly hysterical edge. 'I can't do it any more, Orlando. I need a break. I'm going to Paris, and I'm leaving the baby with you.'

With huge effort Rachel forced a smile for the merchant banker whose hand was creeping rather too low down her back as he whisked her round the drawing room in a clumsy waltz. It was as if Arabella possessed some kind of supernatural power to slow down time, and was making the seconds drag by like hours as Rachel waited for Orlando to emerge from the library.

Not that there was anything to wait for, she thought despairingly. Orlando had only been using her to fill the gap left by Arabella's absence. She'd known that already. If she was any kind of a decent person she'd be happy for him that he'd got his great love back. And, not only that, that he'd got a baby…

She closed her eyes against the sudden rush of tears, but felt them ooze out from under her lids as she pictured Orlando's big, strong hands holding the baby, the lips that had so recently brought her to the brink of ecstasy dropping the tenderest of kisses on that tiny, downy head. And his eyes….his astonishing, glacier-green eyes…looking down into the face of his own child and being softened with helpless love.

As a child she had never known her father, and his absence had caused her to construct an elaborate image of the kind of person she would have chosen to fill his role. A perfect hero: strong, fearless, handsome, honourable. Like Orlando.

She buried her face in the shoulder of the merchant banker while she tried to puncture the misery that was ballooning inside her, but was unable to contain her moan of hopelessness. Unfortunately the merchant banker mistook the sound for pleasure, and instantly tightened his grip, dropping his head to breathe hot, whisky-scented fumes into her ear.

Her eyes flew open in panic and she tried to pull away, but his palm was damp and heavy on her bare back, pushing her body harder against his, so she could feel the pressure of his arousal. It was just like Carlos all over again—and for a second she felt the room tilt and swim as panic swamped her.

'My turn now, I think,' said a cold voice.

Instantly the merchant banker released her from his insistent embrace and melted away. Rachel stood in the centre of the floor, looking dazedly up at Orlando.

His face was ashen, utterly drained of colour and emotion, and his eyes were dark and haunted. For a moment they gazed at each other in wordless agony, before he very slowly placed his bandaged hand on her back and drew her into his arms.

He had rescued her again.

She felt so good. So sweet and uncomplicated after Arabella's savage guile.

The enormity of Arabella's allegation was like a boulder on his chest. It crushed him, so that he wanted nothing more than to thrust it away with all his strength. He didn't trust her.

'Boy or girl?' Rachel whispered.

He held his head very upright, for fear that if he felt her hair brush against him he would be lost.

'Boy.'

'How old?'

'Ten weeks.'

The music of the string quartet was soft and innocuous. Rachel moved with absent-minded fluidity in his arms, so that he could feel her spine flexing beneath his hand. Holding her so close was almost unendurable. Her voice was soft and distant.

'What's his name?'

Orlando's hand tightened convulsively on hers. He closed his eyes briefly.

'Felix.'

He felt her move her head, tilting it backwards so she could look into his face.

'Your brother would be pleased about that, wouldn't he?'

He laughed bitterly. 'Oh, yes. Extremely pleased.'

'Congratulations.'

He shook his head. 'No. Don't say that.' He gave a crooked, humourless smile and echoed her words from yesterday. 'It's not a "congratulations" situation.'

'How can it not be? You have a child…'

'I only have Arabella's word that he's mine.'

He'd always been careful. In those days he'd never been without a wallet full of condoms. Had always used one. Always.

In those days. But not last night. He hadn't used one then.

He swore softly.

Rachel stopped, standing still in the centre of the other dancing couples, in roughly the same bit of floor where he had lain her down less than twenty-four hours ago and lost himself in the miraculous softness of her skin, the evocative rose scent of her hair, the caress of her brilliant hands. Then she had been so uncertain, so vulnerable, but now he could sense her strength.

'She wouldn't lie about something like this, Orlando. Not in these days of…of DNA tests and everything. You're shocked just now—who wouldn't be?—but you have to believe her. You mustn't deny your child a good father. He deserves better than that.'

Neither of them moved. Orlando's face was like granite as he stared straight ahead. His narrowed eyes had darkened to the colour of winter seas, and were opaque with fathomless emotion.

'You're right.' he said slowly, letting his hand fall away from her back. His other hand still held hers, and for a moment he smoothed his thumb across her palm, sending sparks of desire shooting up her arm.

'Thanks for the advice.'

And then he very carefully let her hand go. Without looking back, focusing all his energy on making it to the door, he walked away, taking her words with him as certainly as if she had just carved them on his heart with a rusty nail.

She was right. So right. Little Felix deserved a great father. Which was why Orlando was going to have as little to do with him as possible.

CHAPTER NINE

THE party was coming to an end.

As Orlando walked through the dining room the caterers were clearing tables, and it dimly occurred to him that he hadn't seen Lucinda all night to thank her. He'd had more urgent matters on his mind.

Like his son.

Arabella was in no fit state to look after a goldfish, never mind a baby. The ball-breaking alpha-female whose chilling competence had always terrified the designer pants off the men she worked with had simply collapsed, leaving Orlando no choice but to pick up the slack. Baby Felix would have to stay at Easton while she got herself straight again, and, knowing Arabella, it wouldn't be long before she was with another man…

He stopped beside a table, leaning against it for a moment. He hoped to God it would be someone decent…someone who would stick around. Someone reliable and kind, who would kick a football around with Felix, teach him card games and read him stories. Someone who would be the sort of father Orlando could never be.

He would do everything he could for the child, of course—see that Felix was generously provided for, both in the short term and in his will, ensure that he received the best care and education. But he would do it at a distance. Felix would never have the burden of knowing his blind father.

On the table was a Chinese vase of his mother's, which had

stood in the same place for as long as he could remember. Now it held a dramatic arrangement of tall branches entwined with tiny, twinkling lights. Absent mindedly he reached out and touched one of the branches, thinking it must be something artificial Lucinda had brought from London.

It was rough and brittle. Real. Suddenly he remembered Rachel struggling through the door that afternoon, her arms full of cumbersome branches…

Had *she* done this? He'd sneered at her at the time, but maybe he'd underestimated her.

Briefly he cupped one of the tiny snowflake-shaped lights in the palm of his hand, feeling its warmth, able to see the glow it cast on his skin. It was only small, but the light was surprisingly powerful, and it transformed the stark branches into something beautiful. Something useful.

He closed his hand tightly around it, and the light went out.

For a moment he held it like that. And then he let it go and walked on to say goodbye to his guests.

By the time she finally climbed into bed Rachel ached in every bone of her body, and her face hurt from smiling.

Switching out the light, she lay in the darkness, willing sleep to come but feeling her eyes sting with the effort of keeping them closed. Her breathing seemed too loud, her heartbeat too fast, and her brain couldn't seem to stop endlessly repeating the same tortuous loop of thought, like a faulty recording. She longed for the release of oblivion.

She didn't know how long she lay there before she heard the unmistakable sound of the door clicking open, and watched as a thin sliver of faint light fell across the floor.

'Rachel?'

It was Orlando's voice, and as she replied she knew her own was suffused with a terrible, obvious hope.

Slowly his face swam into focus, a long way above her, ghostly and remote. 'I need your help.'

The hope died instantly. 'Of course…' She got out of bed, noticing that he had carefully stepped backwards to allow her to pass. She swallowed her humiliation and misery. 'What… what's happened?'

As they went out into the corridor she became aware of the distant crying of a baby, which got louder and more insistent as he hurried her through the darkness. As they turned into the front-facing landing it sounded unbearably distressing, and Orlando's fingers, trailing along the wall, fell back to his side and stiffened slightly as he approached a door halfway along the length of the corridor.

He hesitated, as if steeling himself for what lay beyond it, then pushed it open.

Inside, the light was on, and the sudden brightness after the shadowed corridor made Rachel blink. The room was in chaos, and as she stepped over the clothes dropped on the floor she recognised them as Arabella's—the tight black trousers and thin chiffon top she had been wearing earlier. One stiletto-heeled boot lay at an angle beside the bed, as if it had been thrown there hastily as she'd fallen into the bed.

Or been pulled?

With massive effort Rachel averted her mind from the image, and her eyes from mass of dark blonde hair fanning out across the white pillowcase, focusing instead on the scarlet, screwed-up face of the baby beside Arabella. The cries had reached fever-pitch, but she slept on, oblivious.

Rachel stood there helplessly, momentarily unable to think clearly. The noise was all-consuming and urgent, like a police siren, and she cast a panicky glance at Orlando.

He was leaning against the door, his head tipped back, his face utterly expressionless. It was as if he had been turned to stone. Her mouth opened to speak, but she was too shocked to find the words, too distracted by her desperate compulsion to stop the crying. Without thinking she went over to the bed and picked up the baby, holding him awkwardly at arm's length for a moment, before folding him into her body, cradling his head, rocking him, crooning.

'There…there…shhh…shhhhhh…'

Gradually, miraculously, the tiny red face relaxed and the ferocious cries subsided into gulping bleats. Still rocking, still whispering soothing nonsense, Rachel watched the baby's dark eyes fix on her, following the movement of her mouth, watching her intently as fat tears wobbled on his spiky dark lashes.

He was beautiful. She'd never seen a small baby at such close quarters before, and was taken aback by his perfection. Wonderingly she let her gaze travel over his ruff of soft black hair, the slanting, watchful eyes and the lovely mouth that were so heartbreakingly similar to…

'Thank God for that,' said Orlando coldly from the door.

Rachel was unaware that she'd been smiling until she felt that smile die on her face as she looked up at him.

'Oh, my God…' she breathed. 'You bastard. You were so keen to pick up where you left off with *her*—' she tossed a contemptuous look at the inert figure of Arabella in the bed '—that you forgot you had a child to consider. How could you? How *could you*?'

Orlando took a step forward into the room. His face felt like a mask—a hard, brittle mask, behind which he was slowly disappearing. Rachel had totally misunderstood the situation, but there was little point in enlightening her.

'Not easily,' he said coldly, 'when he makes a noise like that.'

'He just needed to be picked up!' Rachel hissed furiously. Orlando saw her lift one hand, shielding the baby's head as if she could protect him from the tension that spat and crackled in the room. 'He probably needs to be fed, for God's sake. Did that not occur to you? Or *her*?' She made a dismissive gesture at the champagne bottle that Arabella must have brought up with her while he was downstairs, dancing with Rachel in his arms. 'Or are *those* the only bottles she's interested in?'

'I'm afraid so,' he said tonelessly, picking up a large black leather bag. 'Milk and bottles are in here, I think. As well as nappies and whatever. Could you do it? I have something important to see to.'

'Important?' she repeated quietly, taking the bag from him. '*Important?* Bloody hell, Orlando, you amaze me. I thought you were…' Awkwardly she hoisted the bag onto her shoulder, trying not to disturb the baby. 'Well, it doesn't matter what I thought. I can see how wrong I was. You're not worthy of being a father. Your heart is made of stone.'

She stormed past him, and when she'd gone he shut the door quietly behind him and went to stand at one of the windows on the landing, looking down into the courtyard below. The candles had all burned out, leaving nothing but shadow. Panic and despair rose inside him, swift and choking, taking him by surprise so that he had to gasp for air.

She was right about one thing. He wasn't worthy of being a father. How could he be when he couldn't see to make up a bottle, couldn't trust himself to carry his tiny son downstairs? But she was wrong about the other. His heart was not made of stone. How much easier everything would be, he thought with savage desolation, if only it was.

A rose-pink dawn was creeping over the snow-covered lawns and stretching tentative fingers into the shadowy kitchen. Sitting uncomfortably in the big Windsor chair, Rachel struggled to keep her eyes open.

In her arms Felix slept peacefully, his pinched face now softened and replete. For long hours she had gazed at it, watching his eyelids flicker, his exquisite mouth twitch into a miraculous tiny replica of Orlando's ironic, crooked smile. His skin was pale, transparent, warmed now by the soft light of the new day, but it was his hands that captivated her most. She watched them flex and curl, as expressive and eloquent as those of his father.

Hovering halfway between sleeping and waking, she found herself unable to think of anything other than Orlando's hands.

She let her head fall against the high back of the chair and felt delicious warmth wash through her as she remembered him undressing her in the moonlight, his fingers moving over her quivering skin, brushing her face, closing over hers as she struggled with his tie…

Her eyes closed, and she was suddenly struck by a vivid image of him walking ahead of her through the gloom, his long fingers brushing the wall, almost as if…

Her head jerked upright, her eyes flying open.

Coming into the kitchen, Orlando walked straight over to the kettle, snatching his hand away as he touched its hot surface. He whirled round.

Rachel was curled up in the big Windsor chair at the head of the long kitchen table. He could see that her knees were tucked up, her head awkwardly resting to one side. He couldn't tell if she was asleep or not, nor see any sign of the baby.

Swiftly he crossed the room, coming to stand over her. As he did so she raised her head, and although he couldn't see her eyes, he could feel them burning into him.

'You should be in bed,' he said gruffly.

There was a small silence, in which he heard her soft, indrawn breath. 'Yes,' she said eventually, with barely controlled anger. 'Yes, I should be in bed. I'd love to be in bed. But that particular luxury was reserved for you and Arabella.'

Orlando turned away and went back to the kettle. He hadn't been to bed, but he didn't tell her that. He'd been up all night, thinking, planning, and had waited until a decent hour this morning to phone an old friend from his RAF days, whose wife was a doctor in a general practice. She had confirmed that it sounded very much as if Arabella was suffering from post-natal depression, and that it would be best for everyone if he supported her decision to have a complete break from the baby.

But she, like everyone else, didn't know of his own medical problems.

'Where is he?' he asked casually, as he switched on the kettle and reached for a mug.

'Here,' she said sardonically, as if she were stating the blindingly obvious.

Fair point, he thought grimly.

Out of the corner of his eye he watched her unfurl her long legs. The baby was nestled against her, and he understood now how she had curled herself around him, cradling him with her body as he slept. Her feet were bare, and she was wearing nothing but the ivory silk nightdress he had peeled off her so hungrily two nights ago.

He felt his heart thud uncomfortably in his chest as guilt, gratitude and a handful of other, far less noble emotions and impulses clashed inside him.

She was standing up now, and he could see the baby's dark head against her creamy shoulder. She must be freezing.

'Why didn't you go back to bed? He's asleep, isn't he?'

She gave an incredulous gasp. 'And do *what*, exactly, with *your son*? Where was I supposed to put him down? You asked me to look after him and I said I would—although believe me I wouldn't have been so accommodating if I'd known it was going to be for half the bloody night! Stupidly, I thought you meant just until one of his parents could tear themselves away from their joyful reunion to come and take over!'

Her furious words exploded and died in the quiet kitchen.

Orlando gave her a cool smile.

'Sorry. It was unreasonable to leave you with him for so long.'

'Too right it was unreasonable! I know nothing about babies. I've never even picked one up before. I didn't know what to do…'

'He doesn't seem to have any complaints.' Orlando nodded curtly at Felix, whose small, starfish hand had come up and grasped a lock of Rachel's hair. He turned away and busied himself with the coffee, to try and distract himself from the sudden surge of acid envy and resentment that rose in the back of his throat. History was repeating itself, he thought with sardonic self-mockery. Felix would be delighted to see his namesake cradled so tenderly in the slender arms of the girl Orlando craved. It seemed the old rivalry was set to run and run.

'He's lovely,' said Rachel softly. 'Which just makes your behaviour all the more despicable. And as for Arabella…'

'She's not well,' Orlando said shortly.

'Wh-what do you mean?'

'Post-natal depression. She's completely unfit to look after a child.' Some sense of loyalty and protectiveness to the baby prevented him from adding that even if she hadn't been ill Arabella felt the same way about babies as most people did about plague-carrying rats.

'She's in a bad way,' he continued blandly. 'The guy she was living with in London dumped her because he suspects the baby isn't his.'

'For crying out loud, he'd be mad not to,' Rachel snapped. 'Look at him, Orlando. Just look at him!' Deftly she moved the baby from her shoulder to the crook of her arm, and crossed the kitchen towards him. 'He's *yours*—can't you *see* that?'

Her voice was raw with contempt, and her words seemed to reach inside him and wrap around his heart, squeezing all the good, honourable, civilised feelings out of him.

'No,' he said very quietly. 'No, I bloody can't.'

There was a long silence. Neither of them moved. He could feel the blood thrumming through him, filling his head with a primitive, insistent pounding. *What had he just said? What the hell had he just said?*

He'd all but told her.

Great. Excellent idea. Tell her. Shock her into leaving or shame her into staying out of pity and guilt. Perfect.

He glanced dismissively down in the direction of the baby. 'I don't see the likeness at all, actually—I'm much taller than he is, for a start—but at the moment that's hardly the point. The fact is, Arabella needs a break. She wants to go to Paris for a while—

she's booked herself into some private spa or something. Which means I'm left holding the baby.'

'Huh!' said Rachel scathingly. 'Don't you mean *I* am...?'

He looked down at her, fixing his eyes on where he thought hers would be, staring into the blackness in the centre of his vision and picturing the luminous amber eyes that had haunted him for weeks after he'd seen that poster. It took all his self-control to keep every trace of emotion out of his voice as he smiled grimly.

'Funnily enough, I was just coming to that.'

CHAPTER TEN

THERE was no more snow in the week following the party. The garden, which had been so suddenly transformed into an enchanted wonderland on the night of Rachel's arrival at Easton, slowly thawed back into damp, grey reality. Like her hopes.

It had been a terrible week, during which she must have asked herself a million times what the hell had made her agree to Orlando's request that she stay on to look after Felix. After all, there were countless compelling reasons for saying no. The fact that she knew nothing about babies might have been a good one to start with.

Straightening up, and tossing another tangle of branches on the pile she had already hacked down, Rachel felt the ache in her shoulders. On the amount of sleep she'd had in the last five days it was perhaps stupid to be out here in the biting cold, making futile attempts to tame the walled garden, but it felt good to be doing something, and the growing mountain of cuttings combined with the ten metres or so of pathway she had cleared gave her a sense of achievement. It also beat staying inside the house, where the atmosphere was several degrees colder than out here in the freezing air.

She paused to survey what she had done so far. With the worst of the brambles and overgrown weeds stripped back, the bones of the formally laid out garden were beginning to emerge. Yesterday she had had the very great excitement of discovering an old stone seat in what had obviously once been some kind of rose arbour. Felix's pram stood there now, and she wandered over and sank down gratefully beside it, looking in at him as she did so.

He was still asleep, thank goodness, his long black lashes sweeping over his flushed cheeks, no doubt exhausted by yet another wakeful night.

He wasn't the only one, she thought ruefully.

After five broken, sleep-deprived nights she was light-headed and spacy with fatigue, aching in every bone and muscle, and more ill-equipped than ever to deal with the constant demands of looking after a small baby. She felt as if she'd been abandoned in the middle of the Amazonian rainforest without a map or a compass. The fact that she wouldn't have known how to read a map or use a compass was almost irrelevant; it was the abandonment that hurt.

Since Arabella's departure, Orlando's withdrawal from both her and the baby had been total.

Looking down into Felix's sleeping face, Rachel felt a stab of anguish. In spite of everything—the torturous nights, the endless challenge of making up bottles and changing nappies— he was utterly adorable. Orlando's relentless refusal to even acknowledge him was as incomprehensible as it was devastating.

She had been so utterly sure that he was better than that. In him she had thought she'd found a man who proved that Carlos's shallowness and her father's fecklessness weren't common to all men. That heroes still existed.

Wrong.

Sadly she tucked the pashmina she had wrapped Felix in more snugly around him, wishing she could keep out the hurt of being unwanted as easily as she could keep out the cold. Impulsively she trailed a caressing finger down his plump rosy cheek, and instantly felt a thud of alarm.

It felt hot. She thought straight away of Lucinda, and the speed with which she'd succumbed to that awful virus. Flu could kill babies, couldn't it? Did Felix have flu?

She took a step backwards, breathing out slowly and trying to quell her mounting panic. Of course he didn't have flu, she rationalised. Lucinda had gone by the time Arabella had arrived; he hadn't even been in contact with her. He felt hot to her because her hands were so cold.

Nevertheless she found herself turning the pram and beginning to hurry back towards the house. He'd slept for longer than usual that morning, but she'd put that down to the two hours he'd been awake in the early hours. She'd fallen into a weary routine at night, bringing him downstairs when he refused to be settled by a bottle, and propping him in his car seat while she played the piano. So far it had never failed to soothe him, and, equally importantly, she found it soothed her too, by giving her something familiar to hold onto. A reminder that she was actually good at something.

Last night she'd played for longer than usual; surely that was why he was sleepy this morning? He couldn't be ill. He couldn't be…

Reaching the back of the house, she hefted the pram over the scullery step and bent down over the sleeping baby. Apart from the hectic flush on his cheeks he seemed fine—his breathing was normal and he was deeply asleep. He'd be crying if he was ill, wouldn't he?

Determinedly she kicked off her boots and walked into the kitchen. She was overreacting, she told herself sternly as she took a pizza out of the fridge and, pulling off its cellophane wrapping, slid it into the vast stainless steel oven for lunch. She was too tired to think straight, never mind make anything more sophisticated. After all, what was the point? Orlando hadn't shown any interest in the things she had taken trouble over. She'd spent all afternoon making laboriously spaghetti Bolognese the other day, and he hadn't even come out from his office to try it.

Wearily she shrugged off the old wax jacket she had pinched from the boot room and went to hang it back up, looking into the pram as she passed. Felix's cheeks were positively glowing now.

Rachel felt an icy jet of adrenaline pulse through her as she pressed the backs of her fingers against his skin.

Her hands were tingling as the warmth seeped back into them, and against them he felt burning hot. She gave him a gentle shake, hoping to see his eyelids flutter open, but they stayed firmly, ominously closed.

'Oh, God,' she whimpered, seizing him and picking him up, still swathed in the pashmina. Clutching him to her chest, she rushed back into the kitchen.

Please, Felix, please…

'Orlando! *Orlando!*'

Startled out of sleep, Felix instantly began to scream, his face turning wine-dark with outrage. Rachel laid him on the table and with shaking hands began to undo the fiddly buttons on his pale blue coat. She needed to get him out of it so she could see him properly, but his back was arched, his small body rigid with fury as he cried.

'*Orlando!*'

God, he really was hot, she thought in panic: his face was burning to the touch now, and as she pulled down the neck of his vest she could see an angry red tide spreading down his chest. Dear God…what was the matter with him?

'Orlando…' she croaked, picking up Felix and holding him against her shoulder, automatically rocking him as blind panic choked her.

'What's wrong?'

He was there in the doorway, and she let out a cry of relief. As he came towards her his face was completely impassive, and in that moment she felt again his strength, the sheer unshakable capability of this man.

'I don't know… It's Felix. I don't know what's wrong with him. I think he's ill. He's so hot, and he won't stop crying, and—' She could hear the hysteria in her voice as she raised it over the noise of Felix's screams, but was powerless to control it.

In one swift movement Orlando's big hands had closed around the angry, bellowing form of his son and taken him from her. For a moment he held him upright, at arm's length, as the baby yelled in rage, and then, cupping one hand under Felix's head, with the other supporting his back, he began to rock him firmly.

Felix blinked, let out a half-hearted hiccupping gulp, and stopped crying, his dark eyes fixed on the face of his father.

The world beyond the steamed-up windows of the warm kitchen faded into a monochrome blur and time hung suspended. The only sound was the low, comforting hum of the fridge; the only movement was the rhythmic rocking motion of the small baby in Orlando's strong, able hands. The angry flush had faded from his cheeks now, and his eyes were bright. Rachel felt she was intruding on a very intimate encounter, but was powerless to tear her eyes away from Felix as his dark, curious gaze met and locked with Orlando's.

And then, with an sudden look of astonished joy and recognition, Felix's face broke into a wobbly smile.

Rachel's hands flew to her mouth. In that instant all the fatigue and frustration, all the confusion and insecurity evaporated, and she found herself torn between laughter and tears.

'He smiled,' she whispered incredulously. 'Orlando, he actually smiled…'

She glanced up and felt the fragile bubble of happiness pop.

Orlando's face was as cold and hard as granite.

'Which just goes to show that he's fine,' he said curtly, thrusting Felix unceremoniously into her arms again. 'Now, if the immediate crisis is over, maybe I could get back to work?'

He was halfway across the kitchen before Rachel found her voice again. Unfortunately sensible words were a little harder to locate.

'God…you…you…. How *could* you? He *smiled*! Don't you understand? That was his *first smile*!'

Orlando didn't flinch. Not a flicker of emotion passed across his perfect face.

'I'm not surprised. He hasn't exactly had much to smile about, has he?'

Rachel gasped as if she'd just been winded. 'You bastard. You absolute, irredeemable *bastard*! It means *nothing* to you, does it? You are so bloody wrapped up in yourself that you can't see what's going on right in front of you!'

Orlando's mouth quirked into a humourless smile at that. 'Interesting. Please, do go on,' he said, very softly.

Rachel tilted her chin and looked at him. 'You're letting him down, Orlando. With every day that passes you are letting your child down more and more spectacularly. And I can't just stand by and watch you do it. He needs you!'

'In that case maybe you'd like to go and talk to the American Chief of Defence about international security issues while I change nappies?' Orlando's voice was quiet, and terrifyingly polite, but there was a lethal edge to it that should have set alarm bells ringing in Rachel's head. But she was too tired, her emotions too raw, to pick up on the atmosphere of dangerous calm that had suddenly fallen.

'International security?' The words flew from her mouth in a rush of scorn. 'Oh, *please*! Forget saving the world for a few days, can't you? What about the security of your *son*? He doesn't need a goddamned superhero; he just needs a father!'

'I see. Is that all?'

His eyes were narrowed to dark, glittering slits, but his face was expressionless. Suddenly his absolute indifference was too much. It was as if a dam had burst inside her and all the frustration and anxiety and anger and longing of the past week had been unleashed in one crashing tidal wave.

'No,' she said through bloodless lips. 'Seeing as you asked, that is not *all*! You told me I lacked courage, and I listened to you—I learned from you—and, boy, have I got braver. Which is why I'm going to say this. *You* lack courage, Orlando. You might have been some hot-shot fighter pilot, you might have risked your life on a daily basis for the service of your country, but only because it made you look good, *heroic*, so that girls like Arabella would throw themselves at your feet and into your bed. Well, good for you. But it's time to grow up now. This is where the real business of being a hero starts—and, you know, it's hard and it's thankless, and it means you have to stay up all night and you don't even get laid. But you have to give your son someone to look up to.'

Orlando stared at her, his head tilted backwards in his habitual attitude of utter disdain.

'That was quite a speech,' he drawled mockingly. 'You've obviously spent plenty of time carefully identifying my numerous shortcomings. Am I to assume that your thorough character analysis includes no redeeming features whatsoever?'

She glared at him as her eyes filled with tears. 'If you'd asked me that a week ago I would have had a very different answer. I thought you were the most astonishingly brave and strong person I'd ever met. But now I can see that I mistook bravery and strength for callousness and coldness.'

He nodded slowly. 'In that case it's just as well I've been looking into making more permanent arrangements for Felix. You'll be delighted to know I've spoken to an agency, and they can have someone here by Monday.'

Rachel stepped backwards, as if she'd been slapped. She could feel the blood draining from her face and her eyes widening in shock.

'No!'

'It'll be better for all of us.'

He turned on his heel, making for the door, but she caught up with him, placing herself and Felix in front of him. 'Orlando, no—you can't! He's had too much change in his life already. He's just got used to me…and—and I've just got used to him!' She was aware that she sounded as if she was pleading, but she was too shattered to care. All she knew was that the thought of leaving Felix was unbearable, and she found herself impulsively reaching out and touching Orlando's arm.

It was a very, very bad move indeed. As her fingertips brushed his skin she almost passed out with longing.

Leaving Felix? If only it was that simple.

'He managed without you before; he'll manage without you again.'

Rachel tried again, feeling as if she was arguing for her life. 'I'm doing OK now, honestly. I can look after Felix just as well as anyone—it's been a tough week, but the worst is over now, and I've learned so much. Especially when you think of how clueless I was when I first arrived—'

She broke off, looking round in alarm, suddenly aware of a horrible smell of burning plastic coming from the direction of the oven. Orlando beat her to it, swearing viciously as he opened the door to release thick clouds of noxious black smoke.

'The pizza!' Rachel wailed. 'But it's not even supposed to be ready yet!'

Swiping ineffectually at the smoke, she grabbed a towel and pulled out the shelf. Melted plastic dripped down between the bars from the polystyrene disc on the base of the pizza, which Rachel had forgotten to remove. Holding it at arm's length, she crossed the room and deposited it in the bin.

When she turned back she saw a flash of grim triumph on Orlando's face.

'You were saying?'

It would be better when she was gone, he thought bleakly as he crossed the hallway. Felix would get used to someone else…someone who didn't cook pizza with the plastic still on, and make damning accusations when she was in possession of only half the facts. Someone who didn't put the radio on and dance with him in the kitchen, or wrap him in her soft, rose-scented scarves, or soothe him when he was fretful in the night by playing Chopin to him in the moonlight.

Orlando's first heroic act had been to let her stay at Easton. His second would be to let her go. Felix would forget. It was just his father who was sentenced to a lifetime of remembering.

CHAPTER ELEVEN

'HUSH Felix…please, darling… It's all right, it's all right…'

Rachel gritted her teeth and tried to make the straps of the car seat meet across Felix's furiously squirming body as his howls intensified, inches away from her ear. With her car out of action, she had borrowed Orlando's to come into the village for supplies, but it was so ridiculously low that she had to virtually bend double to fasten the seat in place. As hostile to babies as its owner, she thought viciously, bashing her head against the top of the car as she stood up.

'Bloody, *bloody* hell!' Rubbing the back of her head with one hand, she picked up a bag of shopping with the other and threw it into the car. It hit the catch of the glove compartment, which fell open, disgorging its contents into the shopping bag. Felix screamed even louder.

Rachel slammed the door, closing her eyes briefly as the noise was abruptly, blissfully, reduced. Since her encounter with Orlando at lunchtime she had felt as she had just before her wedding—filled with helpless dread at what lay ahead. The difference was that then he had been the one to show her a way out. This time he was the cause of her anguish.

But she had come a long way in the last week. It was amazing, she thought miserably, considering Orlando hadn't been talking to her for most of that time, exactly how much he had taught her. The meaning of the word orgasm was one. That she could influence the course of events if she felt strongly enough was another.

And, boy, did she feel strongly about this. She had no intention of just walking away from Felix now. She knew too well what being rejected by your father and growing up in a loveless home felt like.

Making a visible effort to collect herself, she walked round to the driver's side and got in, starting the engine and turning on the radio in an attempt to comfort Felix.

But he was tired and hungry and refused to be soothed. Rachel drove quickly, one hand stroking his cheek, frantically trying to quieten him. But then, as Chopin's *Nocturne in E Minor* came on, filling the small space of the car with memories and longing, she gave up, and they both cried all the way back to Easton.

Rachel longed for an hour-long soak in scented water to calm her frazzled nerves and soothe the ever-present ache in her neck and shoulders, but there wasn't time to bath both Felix and herself before making a start on dinner. She'd discovered that the village boasted an award-winning butcher on the high street, and had thrown herself on his mercy, telling him she needed to cook something foolproof but fantastic. He'd recommended duck, fresh in that lunchtime, and told her exactly what she had to do. She wanted to get Felix settled for the night before making a start.

At the last minute she decided to get into the bath with him, shivering as she stepped into water which, to her, felt only lukewarm. As a tiny concession to vanity she added a dash of her rose-scented bath oil, and, lying back in the chin-deep claw-footed bath, with Felix beached on her chest like a baby seal, she was overwhelmed with anguish and love.

Where would she go if she had to leave here?

Her old life now seemed as remote and unimaginable as snow on a summer's afternoon. Musingly she calculated the date, working out that the concert she had been scheduled to give at the end of her honeymoon was due to take place in just two days.

Idly trickling water on Felix's back, she thought of Carlos. He'd always appeared to her like some evil puppet-master, controlling the world around him as effortlessly as he controlled his orchestra, but surely this situation was beyond even *his* influence? He would have had to cancel the entire tour. The thought gave her a shameful moment of pleasure.

Felix was almost asleep now. Tenderly she gathered him up and stepped out of the bath, wrapping him in a towel and laying him gently on the floor while she slipped back under the water to wash her hair for the first time since the party.

It was hardly the most luxurious beauty regime, but it would have to do. Tonight wasn't about seduction. Tonight was about sense. She wanted to impress Orlando with her maturity and competence—show him she was indispensable, not irresistible. After all, she'd tried that before and it hadn't got her anywhere. He'd managed all too easily to resist her from the moment Arabella had reappeared.

Rinsing the last of the shampoo out of her hair, she sighed and stood up. Even if she'd had all the time in the world there was no point in going to any more trouble anyway. Orlando always looked straight through her.

Downstairs in the kitchen, she set Felix down in his little bouncing chair while she boiled water for his bottle and unpacked the shopping. There was no sign of Orlando, but that was hardly unusual, she thought sourly. Felix was at his most adorable, his hair standing up in a soft dark halo from the bath, his tiny feet in the white sleepsuit kicking excitedly. As she passed she couldn't stop herself from taking them in her hands and raining kisses on him, revelling in the scent of him and in his tiny gasps and gurgles of pleasure.

'You're gorgeous.' She smiled, putting her finger into the palm of his hand and letting him curl his own small fingers around it in a surprisingly strong grasp. 'You're gorgeous and strong and handsome, no matter what your miserable excuse for a father says…. Yes, you are,' she cooed. 'And it's his problem if he can't see it…'

There was a cough from the doorway.

'Sorry to intrude on what's obviously a *private* conversation,' said Orlando acidly, 'but I came to get a drink. Don't let me disturb you.'

Standing up quickly, and disentangling her finger from Felix's octopus grip, Rachel felt a hot rush of colour flood her cheeks. Not that Orlando noticed, of course. He went straight to the fridge and took out a bottle of Sancerre. There was a careful deliberateness about his movements. He looked terribly, terribly tired, she thought, with a sudden flash of compassion which she quickly squashed.

It served him right. He should spend more time with his son and not work such stupidly long hours.

She managed a stiff smile. 'I'm cooking tonight. I hope you can stop work.'

He took down a glass and turned away while he sloshed some wine into it. 'I doubt it,' he said tersely.

It was suddenly very still in the brightly lit kitchen, and Rachel's soft exhalation of frustration and disgust was very audible.

'Fine. Doesn't matter.'

Orlando turned round and leaned against the marble worktop, his eyes boring into her over the rim of his glass. They were as pale as the wine, she noticed with a thud of irritation, feeling a horrible, unwelcome warmth begin to unfurl in the pit of her stomach and spread outwards into her limbs, like wreaths of smoke. His hair was untidy, where he'd been pushing his fingers through it, and there were lines of fatigue around his eyes.

'It's work.'

She busied herself spooning powdered milk into Felix's bottle. 'No problem. I just thought we could…talk. About Felix. But,' she said nonchalantly, 'if you're too busy that's fine by me. I'll eat alone.'

Her body was saying something completely different. His

presence changed the atmosphere in the room, charging it, instantly making the vast kitchen seem too small, too full of his broad shoulders, his penetrating gaze. Oblivious to the currents of hostility swirling around him, Felix gurgled away happily. Rachel was furious to find she'd lost count of how many spoonfuls of milk she'd put in the bottle.

'OK—look, I'll try.' He sighed heavily, making his way to the door, and Rachel felt her chest constrict with annoyance. 'I'll try. Just so long as you promise you're not cooking pizza.'

It was all she could do not to turn round and hurl the tin of powder at him as he left the room, and she allowed herself a small moment of self-congratulation at her admirable restraint.

He hadn't even noticed Felix. Hadn't so much as glanced at him.

Leaving the bottles to cool, she turned and scooped him up, nuzzling her cheek against his soft fuzz of hair. 'Oh, sweetheart, how could he fail to adore you? You're so lovely.' Frowning, she cradled his warmth against her and rocked him absent-mindedly as she finished emptying the shopping bag.

Right at the bottom was a leaflet. She took it out, glancing at it as she went to the bin to throw it away. It must have fallen out of the glove compartment when it had come open.

For a second everything seemed to stop. The clock on the wall, her footsteps across the stone-flagged floor. Her heart. And then it all came rushing back again, with a rushing of blood in her ears. Felix squirmed and whimpered in her arms, and she realised she was crushing him against her as a succession of emotions rampaged through her and understanding dawned.

Her hand shook as she held the leaflet and re-read the title. *Living with Sight Loss. A Patient's Guide.*

At ten past eight Orlando took a deep breath and opened the door of the library. It had been an incredibly exhausting week, with the Middle Eastern border crisis growing more tense and volatile by the minute. His ambitious tactical strategy had, at one point, seemed to be taking fourteen airmen directly to their own funerals, which had tested his reserves of inner strength to their absolute limit.

He'd just heard that the last plane was safely home.

He felt light-headed with relief. Now he wanted nothing more than to go to bed and sleep, deeply, for about a year. Or at least until Monday, when Rachel would be out of the way and he could slide quietly back into his uncomplicated life. His empty, isolated life, free from inconvenient feelings and painful emotions.

Out in the hallway it was quiet, but a surprisingly delicious smell of cooking was drifting through from the kitchen, and he realised with a small jolt of surprise how ravenously hungry he was. Distracted by work, he'd hardly given a thought to food all week, surviving on coffee and snatched slices of toast. He approached the dining room, thinking to walk through it to the kitchen to find Rachel, and came to a standstill in the doorway.

The room was lit with the glow of candles, placed in the old silver candelabra right in the middle of the table and in rows along the mantelpiece, where they were reflected in the mirror. The curtains had been left open, so in the blackness of the windows the candles shone like stars. The light they gave off was surprisingly bright. Soft, gentle, beautiful...but amazingly strong.

Just like the courtyard at the ball.

Which reminded him of several things—most of them in the territory marked *Dangerous*, but one of which was that he'd meant to try ringing Lucinda again. He'd telephoned her office yesterday, only to be told that she was still off sick, but that she'd asked for her sincere apologies to be passed on to him, along with assurances that he wouldn't be invoiced for the party organisation. At the time, he'd thought there had been some mix-up, and had quickly dismissed it. Now, seeing the candlelit room, he wasn't so sure.

Rachel had created those eccentric, stylish arrangements of branches at the ball. What else had she done?

He'd been very quick to dismiss her as being fey and prima-donna-ish, just because she was so very different from Arabella...

Thank God.

Arabella was right. He'd never really loved her, but he'd admired her sharp mind, her well-maintained body and her aggressive high-achieving personality. Looking back on it now, he could see that he'd chosen her in exactly the same way he'd chosen his cars. Quite simply, he always had the best, the fastest, the sleekest model available. It would never have occurred to him to look at anything less, but the fact was that when the terrain had got rough, fast and sleek had been no use to him at all.

And, standing there in the familiar room that suddenly felt so different, he wondered whether if he hadn't been faced with losing his sight he'd ever have seen that. If it hadn't been for the curse of this damned disease everything would be as it was before: he'd still be flying, still with Arabella, and, if she was to be believed, Felix would still be alive. Would he go back?

'I hope this isn't keeping you from anything important?'

Rachel's voice from the opposite doorway was soft and hesitant. He turned his head in her direction, locating her in the dim, flickering light by the coppery gleam of her hair. He felt suddenly absolutely wiped out by the longing to feel it under his hands again.

He shook his head, walking towards her. 'No. It's been a bloody awful week. But the crisis appears to be over.'

'Crisis?'

'Border defence,' he said briefly, following her into the brightly lit kitchen. Going over to the fridge, he pulled out a bottle of champagne. 'We're celebrating.'

'What are we celebrating?'

'Survival.'

Rachel moved to the cupboard to get down glasses as he tore off the foil and effortlessly eased out the cork with his thumbs. His fingers had healed enough for him to have taken the bandages off now, but she could still see the livid dark red scars. Evidence of a more hidden suffering.

She felt unbearably shy, totally unable to look at him and yet paralysingly aware of his nearness. Since she'd read the leaflet things kept coming back to her…slotting inexorably into place—filling in the gaps to make a picture she'd almost known was there all along, from the moment she'd watched him trailing his fingers along the wall as she followed him upstairs. She'd judged him so harshly.

'Here.' Briskly, she took the bottle from him. 'I'll pour this if you could open some red. I should have done it earlier, but I couldn't find the corkscrew.'

He didn't want her to know. She respected that, and she would make it easy for him. God alone knew she'd made it difficult enough already, by repeatedly taunting him for not making enough fuss of Felix. For not being heroic.

She stopped, setting the bottle down for a moment, waiting for the bubbles in the glass to subside again, along with the fizz of remorse and longing that rose up inside her. God, but he was more heroic than she could ever have imagined. To have lost what he'd lost and bear it alone…

She suddenly remembered what he'd said that night when they'd made love. It seemed like a lifetime ago now, like something that had happened to someone else, but his words came back to her just as vividly as if he'd just spoken them. *'I lost something… Something I took for granted. And now I miss it. All the bloody time…'*

Picking up the two glasses, she held one out to him, making sure she put it into his hand.

'To survival.'

'And the end of the crisis?' she suggested quietly, silently cursing the transparent need in her voice.

Orlando took a long mouthful of champagne. 'For the time being,' he said resignedly. 'For tonight, at least, it seems peaceful enough. Tomorrow we can all start thinking of new ways to tear each other apart.'

'Is that how it seems?'

He was looking straight ahead, his eyes glassy with tiredness, a muscle flickering in his cheek. 'Sometimes. It's necessary and inevitable, but, yes. Sometimes I just get tired of planning for the next attack. Always being on the defensive.'

There was a long pause. Rachel averted her eyes from his ravaged, beautiful face and picked up the bottle. She had to have something to do with her hands, otherwise she wouldn't be able to stop herself from reaching up and taking his face between them and smoothing away the lines of exhaustion.

'Shall we go through?'

Orlando set down his glass and dropped his head into his hands while Rachel went back to the kitchen to get the food. He was relieved she'd turned down his offer of help; he was suddenly so overwhelmed with exhaustion he could hardly move.

Which made the effort of getting through dinner without giving himself away extremely unappealing, he thought despairingly. He let his head fall back and closed his eyes.

He heard her come back in. He heard the muffled clink as she put dishes down on the table. But above all that he heard the rustle of her clothes as she walked, the tiny sigh of her breath. And he realised that, despite being so tired he could barely think straight, every nerve was wide awake and taut with awareness of her presence. Her closeness.

He opened his eyes.

'You look shattered,' she said softly. He could hear the smile in her voice, but also the quiet note of anguish, and had to steady himself against it. He could feel his defences slipping, and he couldn't afford to leave himself exposed.

'I'm fine.'

She was leaning over the table, her skin gleaming in the candlelight. She was wearing some sort of dark top, low cut at the front, and he could make out all too easily the dark shadow of her cleavage. He felt his aching body instantly stir into life, and allowed himself a wry smile in the soft gloom. Just as well he couldn't see more. He'd be beyond control if he could.

The smile faded as lust kicked him in the ribs. His sight might be wrecked, but there was nothing wrong with his imagination. Or his memory.

'I hope you're hungry?'

'Ravenous,' he said dryly.

'It's duck. The lovely man in the butcher's shop told me how to cook it and everything, so hopefully I won't poison you, *but—*' She broke off, pausing to suck juice from her thumb before leaning over to take his plate. 'Obviously advising about the meat was as far as his expertise went.' She sounded breathless and apologetic. Orlando found he was smiling.

'Go on…'

'Well…I didn't know what else to cook. Or rather, I did, but I sort of forgot that I'd have to think about other things—I mean, there's a lot of things to think about cooking, and I didn't know how to cook anything else, *so*…' She put another dish in the centre of the table. 'It's chips, I'm afraid.'

Orlando let out a shout of laughter.

'I know, I know, I'm a disaster. And there I was, hoping to impress you with my supreme capability and domestic excellence, and I've blown it. Anyway, I thought if I shredded the duck we could just, you know, help ourselves. I didn't think we'd need knives and forks. Sorry.'

'Don't be.' Orlando lifted his glass to his lips and looked over at her as she sat down. The smile on his face felt unfamiliar. And good. And she'd just saved him from the tedious business of concentrating on cutlery and all the other complicated paraphernalia that waited to catch him out on every formally laid dining table. Which left him free to concentrate on her. 'Duck and chips is my absolute favourite,' he said gravely, leaning over and taking some of the velvety shreds of meat.

'Stop it. I'm trying.'

The light of the candles cast an incandescent aura around her, so he could see the outline of her cheek, the slope and swell of her throat and chest. He felt his throat constrict with sudden, crushing desire.

'I know you are. I'm grateful. And I owe you an apology.'

It was Rachel's turn to mock. 'Yes, you do. Probably more than one. Where would you like to start?'

'Careful,' he said lightly. 'I struggle with the concept of admitting weakness of any kind. It would be a good idea not to push it.'

He heard her soft breath of laughter. 'I see. And what if I tell you it's not weakness? What if I tell you that admitting to being less than perfect is a definite strength?'

He frowned as her words sank in. His voice seemed to have deserted him. Picking up a chip, he ran it slowly around the edge of his plate, soaking up juices from the perfectly cooked meat as he played for time.

No. Don't…

'Well…for a start I underestimated you….assumed the worst.'

'Oh, yes? I don't like the sound of this.'

'I never thought…' he began slowly, then stopped to take a mouthful of wine. Setting down his glass carefully, he gave her an ironic smile and continued. 'I never thought that duck and chips would work so well together.'

'*Orlando Winterton!* If you think that *that* is going to do for an apology, then—'

She broke off abruptly.

'Then what?' he asked quietly. He knew he was straying into dangerous territory, that tiredness was making his defences slip, but it also made it difficult for him to care.

'Then I will be extremely disappointed in you,' she said primly.

Orlando smiled painfully. 'I'd hate to disappoint. OK, I did underestimate you, and as a result I think I owe you a thank you as well as an apology. Would I be right in thinking that last week's ball was orchestrated largely by you rather than Lucinda?'

'No, not at all. She worked amazingly hard. I did hardly anything…'

'I see. Not the flower arrangements?'

'Well, yes. But…'

'Not the candles in all the rooms, and in the courtyard?'

'Yes, I did that, but it was n—'

'It was *great*,' he said with quiet emphasis. 'It was perfect. This house hasn't looked like that for years. It brought it alive again, and I can't tell you how good that felt. It's been empty and dark for a long time.'

'It doesn't have to be.'

Her voice was very low, and he could sense her fear, her hesitancy, and behind it her naked longing. It made him want to get up and drag her across the narrow width of table between them and kiss the living daylights out of her.

For long, long moments neither of them moved. He heard the soft sound of her lips parting, and in the swirling, pulsing darkness in front of his eyes he pictured her tongue moving across them, moistening them…

And then, from the baby listening alarm in the kitchen, Felix's wail cut through the silence.

CHAPTER TWELVE

BURYING her burning face in Felix's milk-scented neck, Rachel gave herself a stern telling-off.

What was she thinking of? She'd set out to prove to Orlando how dependable she was, how capable and sensible. She wanted him to realise she was the best person to look after Felix, and behaving like some rampant nymphomaniac was hardly the right way to go about it.

'I am hopeless, Felix,' she whispered into his soft hair, before placing him back into the creaking depths of the antique Winterton crib. Instantly his mouth opened in a wail of protest.

'Oh, baby,' Rachel said in anguish, 'you mustn't cry. I have to go downstairs. I have to tell your gorgeous daddy that he mustn't get anyone else to look after you.' Felix screwed up his face and cried harder. 'Hush-a-bye, sweetheart. Hush-a-bye…'

It was no good. Sighing, Rachel scooped Felix up and held him against her shoulder, rocking and soothing with quiet desperation. 'I've already messed up with the food… Please little one, *please*…I need to talk to him. It might be the only chance I get… It's for your sake, you know. I can't bear the thought of leaving you…' She paused, pressing a kiss onto the top of Felix's head, and, dropping her voice to a whisper, added, 'Or him. I can't bear the thought of leaving him either…'

Standing at the window, she drew back the curtain an inch and gazed out into the darkness. There was no moon tonight, and the garden was shrouded in blackness. A hundred shades of black. She thought of the path she had discovered, the stone seat that had been hidden by tangled undergrowth and years of neglect. There was so much here that she wanted to do, so much that she had already grown attached to.

And at the centre of it all, dark and compelling, was Orlando.

On her shoulder Felix snuffled and hiccupped. Rachel felt his head lift questingly, and realised with a sinking heart that he wasn't going to go back to sleep without a bottle.

She sighed. 'Oh, sweetheart… You're as stubborn as your father. I give in.'

'You shouldn't,' said a low voice from behind her. 'You're far too nice for your own good. You should stand up to both of us.'

Cupping Felix's head, she whirled round.

She could see nothing but Orlando's silhouette against the light from the doorway behind him, his broad shoulders filling the space.

'Ah.' She sighed, turning back to face the dark garden again, swaying gently and rubbing the baby's small, curved back. 'I tried that earlier, remember? You asked me to leave.'

He waited for a heartbeat before answering. 'Not as a punishment.'

She could feel him behind her. A little way away, not close. But close enough for her skin to tingle with awareness and her stomach to tighten. She spun slowly round to face him. 'That's how it feels,' she said bleakly as her eyes filled with tears. 'That's exactly how it feels. And I know it's unreasonable, and it's my own stupid, stupid fault, but I've fallen in love with this boy…'

With a stifled sob she shifted Felix gently from her shoulder to settle him in the crook of her arm. He gazed up at her, his eyes dark and gleaming.

'I know I had no right, because he's not mine—he belongs to Arabella, and to you, but he's so lovely I couldn't help it. I didn't want it to happen. I wish it hadn't—'

'Don't say that.'

'But it makes it all so much more painful. I was supposed to be persuading you tonight to let me stay—proving to you that I was capable and efficient and the ideal person to care for Felix. But I've messed it up by forgetting to cook vegetables and crying *again*. No wonder you've found someone else to look after him, since most of the time I've spent in your company I seem to have been in floods of ridiculous tears.'

'Not ridiculous. It's been a pretty intense week. And anyway, that's not the reason I found someone else.'

'Then why?'

'I'm trying to break the habit of a lifetime and think of what's best for someone else for a change.'

His voice was as harsh and bleak as a Siberian dawn. Rachel bit her lip as a fresh tide of tears filled her eyes. She should be pleased that he was thinking of Felix, that he wanted what was best for him. It was awful of her to be so selfish.

She swallowed. She had to respect his right to make decisions for his son. Hell, there had been enough times over the last week when she had been desperate for him to show that even he'd noticed him. Maybe if she knew that he was going to be more involved she wouldn't mind leaving so much. If she just knew that Felix was going to be loved...

'Just promise me...' she said in a shaky voice. 'Promise that whoever looks after him will love him. I know he needs someone who'll know all about weaning and getting him into a proper sleep routine...'

She was momentarily distracted by Orlando's soft exhalation of amusement.

'You mean someone who'll know how to get him back to sleep without a personal Chopin recital every night?'

'Exactly—someone efficient and organised. But someone who'll love him too.'

'Arabella's efficient and organised. I'm not sure the ability to be loving and patient exists alongside those qualities.'

At some point, she couldn't say how or when, they had come

closer together, so that now they were standing with Felix almost cradled between them. Their heads were bent downwards over him. With a wrenching sensation inside Rachel remembered that Orlando couldn't see the way Felix's dark eyes shone in the dim light, the contours of his beautiful mouth. She took a deep, shaky breath.

'He's so like you, Orlando,' she said with quiet deliberation. 'His eyes might be blue, not green, but they darken like yours when he's cross or upset... And it's there in the shape of his mouth, with its perfect cupid's bow upper lip, and in his dark, arched eyebrows, and even in his hairline...'

It was a risk, she knew that, and the stakes were high. Orlando Winterton was the proudest, most remote person she had ever met; the barriers he had placed around himself were high and un-breachable. Slowly, hesitantly, she groped for his hand in the darkness and, taking it in her trembling one, brought it up to Felix's head.

She looked up at him. He was standing with his head tipped back in that way that she had always taken to be indicative of disdain, but which she now understood was to enable him to make the most of his limited field of vision. In the half-light his face was shadowed and impossible to read.

Anxiety twisted inside her. If she got this wrong she could lose everything, but since she was going to end up doing that anyway it hardly mattered. If her instinct proved right, Felix might just end up with a father.

'Even his hands are like yours. He's got your long, tapering fingers, and your beautifully shaped fingernails.'

Orlando hadn't moved his hand. It still rested against Felix's cheek, and Rachel watched, mesmerised, as his thumb very lightly caressed the whisper-soft hair at his temple. When she lifted her gaze she saw that the expression on Orlando's face was one of exquisite agony.

'I'll make a promise to you,' she whispered hoarsely. 'I promise that I'll go quietly—no more arguing or pleading—if you'll just show me that the person who will look after Felix and love him will be you.'

Orlando's head whipped sideways, as if she'd slapped him. He spoke through gritted teeth.

'I can't.'

'You can.' She kept her tone low, determined. 'You have to work, so of course you need the person from the agency to do all the day-to-day stuff, but you can be the one who *loves* him, the one he loves back and looks up to…'

He gave a low gasp of exasperation and pain and shook his head.

'Not going to happen…'

Rachel took a deep breath. 'Well, if you won't, I'm not leaving.' Then, heart pounding, she handed Felix to him.

'Think about it while I get his milk.'

Orlando took his son, his gaze fixed glassily ahead as Rachel silently left the room.

He didn't look down. He didn't have to.

Rachel had described him so lovingly that even without trying to fix his ruined gaze on something above Felix's face in order to bring it into the edge of his sight he could picture him. Maybe it wasn't accurate, maybe it owed a lot to countless dusty albums full of remembered pictures of himself and his brother as dark-eyed, dark-haired babies, but it had made his child real.

As if to emphasise this fact, Felix uttered a soft, clear sound that reached right into Orlando's heart and wrapped itself around it. He dipped his head, closing his eyes as his mouth brushed the top of the baby's downy head and breathed in. He smelt of baby powder and roses, and Orlando felt a knife turn in his ribs.

In the past nightmarish week his careful defences had been battered by a succession of powerful emotions. But he was used to keeping emotion at bay. He was a defence expert, for God's sake. He knew all the tricks.

Keep information on a need-to-know basis. To the point. Impersonal.

But she'd really got him now, hadn't she? Somehow, without him even noticing she had simply dissolved all his barriers until his heart lay exposed—as defenceless as the child in his arms.

God, for the first time in a year he felt almost human. Downstairs, sharing a meal in the candlelight he had forgotten, actually forgotten, that he wasn't *the person he used to be*, as Arabella had put it. Suddenly that person had ceased to matter. He was himself now, and Rachel had made him that.

But with humanity came pain. He could feel it now, crouching in the velvet darkness around him, waiting. He could open his heart to Felix, and take on the anguish of knowing he would never be a proper father, or he could keep him at arm's length, and as a punishment have to endure the torture of having Rachel close but impossibly forbidden.

Orlando Winterton was no stranger to suffering. But losing his sight was like a paper cut compared to the agonising prospect of losing his heart.

Rachel stood in the doorway, frozen with indecision, the bottle in her hand.

Orlando stood over the crib, Felix in his arms, his astonishing, heroic face lined with anguish. She longed to go to him, was almost bent double with the rush of longing that swept through her as she let her gaze travel over his massive shoulders, with their sense of restrained power, and down his strong arms to where Felix's small head nestled in his elbow.

She longed to go to him but she didn't want to intrude. This was what she'd hoped for. She couldn't break the moment now.

So she stayed where she was, watching in silent hope and fear and longing as Orlando lifted Felix higher in his arms and dropped a kiss onto the top of his head.

Maybe she did make a sound, because the next thing she knew he was looking towards her. Had she not known, she would never have picked up the almost imperceptible note of uncertainty in his low voice.

'Rachel?'

She went forward into the room. 'Here's his milk.'

'You do it.'

'Uh-uh. You have a magic touch—he's almost asleep already. If I take him he'll wake up again.' She put the bottle in his hand. 'Look—you just hold it for him like that, and he's clever enough to take it for himself…' Felix's little questing mouth found the teat of the bottle and sucked powerfully. Rachel watched surprise flicker over Orlando's shadowed face as he felt the tug, and then she quickly turned away, walking over to the bedside table and turning on her iPod, unleashing the first shimmering notes of Chopin's *Nocturne in E Minor* into the room.

Orlando's mouth twitched into a smile. 'I thought he preferred a live performance?' he murmured, so quietly that she had to go and stand beside him to catch what he was saying.

'I guess I'd be lying if I pretended I only played for his benefit,' she whispered apologetically.

He frowned. 'You miss it?'

'Of course. It's been my life for as long as I can remember. It's like losing a part of myself.' Suddenly she realised what she was saying, and stopped just in time. 'Oh…' she breathed in relief. 'He's asleep…' Gently she took the bottle from Orlando. 'You put him down. I'll be outside.'

She left quickly, before he could argue. Waiting on the landing, she listened intently, praying that Felix wouldn't choose this moment to do one of his amazing instant wake-ups.

He didn't. A few moments later Orlando came out and pulled the door half shut. As he turned round Rachel saw with a shiver that the barriers were back in place. His face was perfectly blank. She stepped forward.

'You see? You did it. You did it brilliantly. You fulfilled your side of the promise, and so now I have to fulfil mine.' She was trying hard, so very, very hard, to keep the break from her voice. 'You've shown me that you'll love him and look after him, so now I have to do as I promised and go quietly.'

'No. *No*.'

He took a step towards her, pulling her into his arms with something like desperation. He heard her cry out in sorrow and longing in the instant before his mouth found hers, and he felt her need as forcefully as he felt his own. It was agonising, impossible to endure, when the prospect of release was so within reach—like withholding drugs from an addict; he knew it was for his own good, but, God, he didn't care any more. At some point this evening he had gone way, way beyond caring about what might happen to him in the future, or about anything that he had been or felt in the past.

Everything was simple. He wanted Rachel. He wanted the firelight and the candleglow and the warmth and her vibrant, blazing hair. He was tired of endless darkness and cold.

'Orlando—' She tore her mouth from his, and he felt her hands push his face from hers, holding him at arm's length. 'I can't—'

She had been going to say that she couldn't settle for just one night, but the words died on her swollen lips as she looked into the indescribable green of his eyes and knew that she could. Whatever he was offering, she would take it. If she had to leave him tomorrow it would be better to have something to hold on to, to remember, than nothing.

'Rachel?' His voice was sharp, his eyes blazing into hers searchingly, and she had to remind herself that he couldn't see her, couldn't read the blatant longing in her face.

'I can't help wanting you,' she said in a hoarse whisper, dropping her gaze from his tortured face and pressing her mouth to the hollow at the base of his throat.

'I know.' It was a moan of despair. 'I've tried, but I'm lost…'

'Then we're lost together,' she sobbed, reaching up to pull his mouth back to hers, breathing in the scent of him, feeling the hardness of his stubble-roughened jaw against her palms. They stumbled backwards, and then she felt him grasp her hands, and he was pulling her along the corridor, quickly, urgently, until they both broke into a run.

They turned a corner into the front landing, where there were no lights on, and the inky shadows enveloped them. Rachel's footsteps slowed uncertainly and Orlando turned, taking both her hands in his strong, sure ones, drawing her forward.

'You're afraid of the dark?'

She stopped, her hold on his hands tightening, so he couldn't help but be pulled back to her. 'Not when I'm with you,' she said throatily, standing on tiptoe to reach his ear.

The low note of desire in her voice seemed magnified in the blackness. A second later Orlando was scooping her into his arms and striding down the remainder of the corridor to his room. Kicking open the door, he hesitated just inside the threshold to find her mouth with his, and her hand went up to hold his head, sliding across the hard plane of his cheek until her fingers were entwined in his hair, pressing him deeper into her.

He let her slither from his arms, setting her back on her feet so his hands were free to explore and reveal. The room was velvet black, and they were both sightless; he could feel her hands clumsily seeking the buttons to his shirt, fumbling to work them free. Her own shirt was soft, clinging perfectly to her narrow body, and without hesitation he swept it over her head.

He groaned as his hands found the rose-petal perfection of her skin, dropping his head hungrily to the silken dome of her shoulder, scraping his teeth against it, feeling the powerful shudder of desire that shook her as he trailed his fingers around her ribs to the fastening of her bra. Helplessly she grabbed his shirt in her fist, twisting it, pulling…

'I can't… Orlando—take it off.'

He pulled it over his head and she heard the soft sound it made as it landed on the floor at their feet. She took in a shivering gasp. For a moment they stood inches apart, unable to see each other but exquisitely aware. Then Rachel took a small step towards him, so that her nipples skimmed his bare chest. It was all she could do not to cry out in devastating ecstasy as she heard his indrawn breath and felt his head tip backwards.

It was the point of no return. Grasping her shoulders in both hands, he crushed his mouth down on hers, and she felt herself dissolving, disappearing into the chasm of yearning that she'd been tiptoeing around all week. She didn't know how they made it onto the bed, how the rest of their clothes disappeared, was only aware of the feel of him under her damp thighs, the hardness of his jutting hip bones, the concave sweep of his stomach, ridged with muscle, and beneath that the smooth, hard length of his erection. She was kneeling up, over him, and his hands came up to hold her steady, spanning her ribs, measuring, discovering, moving reverently over her breasts, her collarbone…

He was *seeing* her, she thought hazily. And that was her last coherent thought as she gripped him with her knees, rising up to take him inside her, and abandoned herself to blissful sensation.

CHAPTER THIRTEEN

IN DREAMS Orlando could always see perfectly again.

Falling into a deep, grateful sleep for the first time in days, with Rachel's head on his chest, he saw her properly. She was wearing her wedding dress, as she had had when she'd arrived at Easton and got out of the car with her vivid hair blowing around her like a pennant, and as she walked towards him her amber eyes were incandescent with love.

The picture was shattered as the telephone on the bedside table began to ring.

Rachel felt Orlando move beneath her, the sonorous beat of his heart fading from her head as a shriller sound took its place.

The phone.

She felt a dart of alarm. Telephones ringing in the middle of the night were only ever bad news weren't they? But every inch of her was still blissed out and glowing from Orlando's touch, and the outside world still seemed a long, long way off. With Orlando she felt safe.

In the darkness she could dimly make out the sweeping arc of his arm, moving over her to pick up the telephone, could feel the flex of his muscular chest beneath her cheek. She found she was smiling as she listened to his husky sleep-drenched voice.

'Orlando Winterton.'

And then she felt the smile dissolve from her face as he sat up. Moving sideways onto the cold pillow, she heard him swear viciously. She could just make out the muscles moving beneath the skin of his broad back as he thrust a hand into his hair. When he spoke his voice was steely.

'*Hell*. How is she?'

Rachel's heart had begun to thud uncomfortably, and the heavy contentment in her limbs had been replaced with icy pin-pricks of dread. She could hear the voice on the other end of the phone, but not make out what it was saying. It sounded ridiculously tiny and innocuous; how bizarre that it could shatter her brief moment of happiness.

'What do you mean, you can't tell me?' Orlando got up angrily. For a moment she caught a brief glimpse of his magnificent body before it melted, ghost-like, into the blackness of the huge room and she was left with nothing to do but listen.

'I know I'm not her next of kin…but I'm the *father* of her *child*, for God's sake!'

So. There was no mistaking to whom he was referring. Or the anxiety in his voice.

Quietly Rachel slipped out of bed and found her way back to her own room. Without Orlando the darkness of the old house frightened her—but not nearly as much as the emptiness inside herself.

'She's in hospital. They won't tell me any more, other than that she's asking for me. I have to go.'

Rachel nodded wordlessly and, balancing Felix on one arm, collected up the breakfast cups and plates with the other. In the grey light of early morning, Orlando looked utterly shattered, his narrow, slanting eyes shadowed, his face gaunt and pale. How pathetic of her foolish heart to want so desperately to fold him into her arms when all that anguish was for someone else.

Bloody Arabella.

'I've made phone calls. All the Paris flights are booked up until this evening, so I've called in some favours with the RAF. We leave from Northolt at eleven.'

Rachel's head snapped round. 'We?'

Orlando sighed and pushed a hand through his hair. 'Sorry. I should have asked. She'll want to see Felix, so I'd like you to come with me.'

It was a measure, thought Rachel desolately, of her utter enslavement to him that she only could feel relief. How astonishingly humiliating. She was actually *glad* to be accompanying him to the bedside of the woman he loved, because being left behind without him was too terrible to contemplate.

'OK.' She gave a wan smile. 'I'll go and get some things together.'

Orlando got up from the table and pushed his chair in with a violent scraping sound that set his teeth on edge. What was one more lie to add to the sprawling web of deception that his life had somehow become? he thought viciously. Arabella hadn't asked to see her son; she wouldn't be so selfless. No. Orlando wanted Rachel to come for far less noble reasons.

Because he couldn't face the journey on his own.

And because he was terrified that if he left her she wouldn't be there when he got back.

George drove them to the airport in Lord Ashbroke's old Daimler. Orlando sat in the front, with Rachel in the back, beside Felix in his car seat. As they drove through the high gateposts she turned round and gazed at Easton through the rear window, wondering when she would see it again.

If she would.

And, if so, under what circumstances.

For one difficult, painful, wonderful week she had felt as if it was her house, and she had allowed herself to care for it just as she cared for Felix. She had invested something of herself there as she had pottered about in that bright kitchen and torn her hands on brambles in the old walled garden.

The thought of Arabella returning as mistress of Easton was unbearable.

The only thing that was worse was the thought of her returning as mistress of Orlando.

There was what seemed to Rachel to be an entire uniformed squadron waiting to greet them on the tarmac as they pulled up alongside the small but luxurious plane. Orlando Winterton was certainly *somebody*, she realised, watching him from under lowered eyelashes as crewman after crewman saluted him. Not a flicker of emotion crossed his face. However, as the engines started and the plane began to gather speed along the runway, she noticed that his knuckles showed bone-white through his skin as his hands gripped the armrests of the cream leather seat.

'Last night…' She was looking straight ahead, and so missed the fleeting pained expression that crossed Orlando's face. 'Last night when you asked me whether I missed the piano… You knew the answer already, didn't you? Because that's how you feel about giving up flying?'

'Yes.'

It was impossible to explain that feeling. He missed it viscerally. It had been so much a part of who he was, and defined the part of him that had died that day in Andrew Parkes's office—the heroic, risk-taking, thrill-seeking part.

He closed his eyes briefly, tensing himself for the question that would inevitably follow. *Why did you give it up?*

But she said simply, softly, 'I can understand why. It must be an incredible feeling.'

Relief washed through him, but it was tinged with despair. Last night, when he'd kissed her in the corridor outside Felix's room, he'd crossed a line. That was the moment when he'd accepted that he wanted her…not just at that moment, but for longer. For ever. But he hadn't even told her the truth about himself yet.

He had to, of course. Soon. But…

God. How ironic. He was *afraid*. He, who had berated her from the moment they met for her own lack of courage, was frightened. And she had shown, time after time, that she was brave in ways he was only just discovering.

'It is. There's nothing like it,' he said gravely.

But that wasn't true either. Last night—with her hands in his hair, her mouth on his mouth, her legs around his waist—*that* had felt like flying, with the light coming up over the horizon and the dew forming rainbow diamonds on his wingtips. Holding her as she'd shuddered and cried out in his arms…*that* had felt like flying home into a clear pink and gold dawn.

The car that awaited them was long, black and impossibly shiny. It reminded Rachel very much of a hearse—which, given her mounting sense of dread, seemed horribly appropriate.

It was as if for the past week she and Felix and Orlando had lived in a sort of Eden, cut off from the rest of the world at Easton Hall. It had hardly been idyllic…most of the time she had felt lonely, confused and isolated…but it was only now that she realised how much strength and comfort she had gained simply from knowing Orlando was nearby. Looking back, she suddenly saw the days that had passed there as peaceful and sheltered, and the nights when she had played the piano into the listening darkness as magical.

As they inched their way through the Paris traffic she felt totally unprepared to return to reality. The world beyond the tinted glass of the car window seemed loud and aggressive, full of busy, indifferent people and glaring, garish sights and sounds. She sank back into the leather upholstery, closing her eyes and mentally searching for something to counter the assault of unfamiliarity and hostility. It was a trick she had been taught by one of her piano teachers, to calm herself down before a performance. All she had to do was pick an image and concentrate on it very hard, carefully filling in all the sensory details…

Standing holding Felix in the semi-darkness with Orlando. Close to him…looking down at Felix. Reaching out, feeling for Orlando's hand, her skin brushing his—feeling its warmth, the reassuring heaviness and solidity of his hand, hearing the whisper of skin against skin. Breathing in…slowly, steadily…the

*smell of warm, babymilk softness...and beneath it, like a
haunting, bass note, Orlando's dry, masculine scent. Lifting his
hand, bringing it up to Felix's head, raising her gaze to
Orlando's face...*

He breathing quickened, and she felt her heart-rate double as
her mind, too far advanced down that particular track, refused to
be called to heel. But then she was aware of other things—of the
car slowing, making a sweeping turn, coming to a standstill.

She didn't want to open her eyes. She didn't want to let
reality back in.

'This is the hospital.'

The tableau of the couple with the baby in the darkened room
faded, and she slowly opened her eyes.

Orlando was reaching for the door handle. She watched his
long, elegant fingers deftly move along the walnut inlay of the
door to locate it and, once they'd done so, hesitate. He turned his
head back towards her.

'I don't know how long I'll be. It's best that you go on ahead.
I'll send a message to the hotel if she's up to seeing Felix.'

His eyes seemed very dark, opaque with emotions Rachel
didn't want to think about. Feelings that had nothing to do with
her and everything to do with the woman he was just about to
see. There was a moment...a long, shimmering moment of
unspoken possibility...when she wanted to find something to say
that would sum up a fraction of what she was feeling. She didn't
blame him for going to Arabella. She knew out of the two of them
the other woman had the greater claim, she had never been led
to believe anything else. It was just that she would have liked, in
this last few seconds before he opened the door and was swallowed up by the outside world again, to tell him how much it had
meant to her, this enchanted time. How very, very much.

He turned his head, so she could see him in profile. She caught
the movement of his throat as he swallowed. She bit her lip hard,
knowing that if she were to speak the only words that would
come out would be *I love you.*

And then it was too late. He threw open the door and the world came rushing in, with a blast of sleet-edged air and a cacophony of city noise. Rachel watched him get out of the car in one lithe movement, his broad shoulders shielding her from the worst of the damp and cold for a second before he stood aside.

Her mouth opened in horror.

It was like an explosion inside her, spreading quickly outwards as the information was relayed to different parts of her body. There was a split second when it was just her eyes that registered the large poster on the building behind Orlando, advertising a concert that was taking place tomorrow night, and then the rest of her body caught up, going into full shock response as she stared at her own smiling face.

Orlando leaned back into the car—coming between her and Rachel Campion, concert pianist.

'We need to talk,' he said gruffly.

Rachel didn't answer. Her mind was in uproar. Craning her head to look past him, she looked again to see if, in her shock, she had initially missed the part that said the concert was cancelled. Surely Carlos and her agent and the PR people should have publicised the fact that it wasn't going ahead by now?

'Rachel, please…' Orlando's voice was infinitely weary and seemed to come from a long way away. 'I'm sorry to bring you all this way and abandon you like this… Look, I promise we'll talk later.'

'What? Oh. OK…'

Orlando's face darkened. She sounded utterly distant, utterly preoccupied. He'd spent the entire journey feeling absolutely eaten up with remorse for his emotional cowardice, steeling himself for this moment. He'd tried to bridge the chasm that he'd created around himself—only to find that she wasn't remotely interested in crossing it.

He straightened up and slammed the door, then waited until the car had pulled slowly away before he turned and went slowly up the steps to the hospital.

His head ached. Away from the familiarity of Easton, his reduced sight made every small thing a grinding challenge, so that just finding his way down the labyrinth of corridors towards the ward he was directed to triggered the same adrenaline surge he'd used to get during dangerous night-time search patterns over the North Sea.

He came to the end of a corridor, where it opened out into another high, elegant hallway. At the end was a desk. The nurse greeted him by name as he approached.

'Ah…Monsieur Winterton? It's good that you're here. Mademoiselle de Ferrers has been asking for you.'

'How is she?'

'Well, physically she is improving, there is no reason why we shouldn't discharge her in the next day or so, though mentally we are…concerned.' Orlando detected a distinct edge of frosty disapproval in her tone. 'She is finding it very difficult to come to terms with the fact that she will be scarred.'

Orlando felt as though an icy hand had closed around his throat. 'Was it a car accident? Was she driving?'

The nurse had picked up a clipboard and was examining it. 'No, *monsieur*. She had cosmetic surgery,' she said tonelessly. 'A breast-lift at an unregistered clinic in Switzerland. The surgeon was not aware that she had so recently had a child. It was too soon to do any kind of procedure, and unsurprisingly she suffered severe infection. She checked in here two days ago, and our doctors have done their best, but the scars may never disappear.'

The icy sensation dissolved, and was replaced by the much more familiar one of slow, burning anger. He managed a stiff smile.

'Thank you for your help. Now—may I see her?'

CHAPTER FOURTEEN

THE car door was opened and Rachel got out stiffly. The hotel in front of her looked a lot like Buckingham Palace, she thought dimly. Or how Buckingham Palace would look if it had been made over by Parisian designers: authentically period, but at the same time outrageously cutting-edge and chic.

Perhaps to ensure she didn't create a bad impression in the highly polished reception hall, in her faded jeans and ancient cashmere sweater, she was ushered straight to a room by a porter who looked as if he'd just stepped out of an advert for Armani suits in French *Vogue*. He carried the car seat as if it were an un-exploded bomb, while in it Felix grizzled, and Rachel followed wordlessly, her mind so taken up with questions and suspicions that she hardly noticed the splendour of the halls and corridors they passed through.

What was Carlos up to?

Having delivered her to a suite the size of the average family home, the Armani porter dissolved away again. Rachel picked up Felix and looked slowly around her. The room in which she was standing was straight from a film set. Four tall sets of French windows opened out onto a wrought-iron balcony, each set framed by excessive amounts of sumptuous swagged silk. The walls were painted pale gold and inlaid with silk-damask panels, and the furniture was upholstered in the same shades of gold and ivory. The overall effect was swanky interior design magazine meets Madame Pompadour. Rachel wasn't sure if she ought to be wearing a crinoline and a powdered wig, or designer hotpants and a feather boa.

The air was heavy with the scent of the hot-house flowers which were placed in fleshy arrangements on every polished surface. Opening a door at the far end of the room, she found herself facing an enormous bed, over which a cascade of grey and gold striped silk spilled down from an antique corona of twisted gilt leaves.

Miserably she surveyed it. It was almost indecently romantic—a bed for making joyous, decadent love in, she thought dully, for spending lazy, lust-drenched afternoons in and drinking vintage champagne…preferably from each other's navels.

She turned away sharply as her mind veered straight back to last night, and her body obligingly provided an instant sensory replay. Darts of remembered bliss fizzed along her nerve endings as she recalled how he'd held her, running his brilliant, beautiful hands over her body, unleashing a storm of desire in her that had been almost violent in its intensity.

And the worst bit was, she couldn't be sorry. Even knowing what she knew now, even being here, on her own in the most romantic city in the world, while he went to the bedside of the woman he loved, she couldn't regret what they'd done.

Jiggling Felix absent-mindedly, she found herself standing in front of another closed door. She pushed it open, expecting perhaps a bathroom, and felt tears of self-pity spring to her eyes as she took in what it was.

Another bedroom, small and narrow this time, with a single bed covered in sensible blue and white check.

He'd booked a two-room suite. This must be her room.

The short, grey day was already giving way to night. Rachel had carefully measured out the afternoon by playing with Felix and giving him an early and much drawn out bath in the exquisite temple-like atmosphere of the *en-suite* bathroom, grateful for the sound of his squeals and gurgles in the oppressive atmosphere of such luxury. All the time her confused brain had ricocheted between tormenting thoughts of Orlando, sitting at Arabella's bedside holding her hand, and needling thoughts of Carlos.

Eventually, driven to distraction by the incessant questions hurtling around her brain like leaves caught in a whirlwind, she seized the telephone and dialled Reception, nervously stammering out an enquiry about the concert that was being advertised and the possibility of obtaining tickets. There was a pause, during which she could only just hear the concierge tapping details into a computer over the hectic hammering of her heart, before he came back to say he was very sorry, but the concert was all sold out.

'It is still going ahead, then?' she confirmed weakly.

The voice at the other end sounded surprised. *'Oui, mademoiselle.'*

Rachel had only just replaced the receiver when the phone rang again. Thinking it was the concierge, telling her he'd enquired further and had discovered he was mistaken, she grabbed it eagerly. But this time he was telling her that a car was waiting for her downstairs.

The first thing she saw, before she'd even set foot in Arabella's room in the hospital, was Orlando. He was asleep, stretched out on a square and uncomfortable-looking sofa opposite the doorway, with one arm falling to the floor like in the pre-Raphaelite painting of *The Death of Chatterton*.

Rachel stopped on the threshold as her heart jolted painfully against her ribs. Seeing him there gave her an extraordinary, powerful feeling of homesickness as well as longing. After the lonely hours in the gilded splendour of the hotel, the unfriendly city streets, in the strangeness of the hospital he looked achingly familiar. His head was thrown back, his dark hair falling away from a forehead that, in sleep, was smoothed of all its anger and its anguish. His beautiful lips were slightly parted, and one hand rested on his chest, his palm upturned, his fingers slightly curled.

Without thinking she crossed the room and, setting down Felix in his car seat, let her gaze travel over Orlando. There was a bone-deep ache inside her as she watched the slow rise and fall of his chest, the languid, almost imperceptible pulse in his neck. On the hand which lay across his chest she could see the still-raw scars on his fingers, and she was instantly transported back to the kitchen, to the breathless moment when she'd held him and his blood had run into her own hands and she'd felt his pain. She couldn't stop herself from reaching out to touch him…

The next moment she almost jumped out of her skin as an amused, mocking voice came from the direction of the bed.

'Darling, forgive me for intruding on this private act of worship, but I don't believe we've met properly.'

Rachel whirled round. 'Oh! Sorry! I was just…I mean, I didn't…' She was blushing furiously, aware that whatever she said was just going to make the situation worse. 'Sorry. I'm Rachel.'

Arabella was sitting up against a mountain of snowy pillows, wearing a silk wrap beneath which Rachel could just see bandages covering her chest. Aside from that, she didn't look ill at all. The eyes that were regarding Rachel so shrewdly were subtly made up with mascara and shadow. Through the fog of her humiliation Rachel noticed that they didn't even flicker in Felix's direction.

Arabella's immaculately glossed mouth spread into a slow, incredulous smile. It was as if she had suddenly come across a winning lottery ticket in an old handbag. *'Rachel,'* she said wonderingly. 'Yes, of *course*. How *amazing*.'

'Amazing? I'm sorry…I don't know what you mean?'

Arabella gave a soft laugh, but her narrowed eyes never left Rachel's face. 'You're too modest, Rachel. Far too modest. Here was I, thinking you were some sweet local girl Orlando had unearthed at Easton, but you're not, are you? Far from it—you're *Rachel Campion*, concert pianist and, according to those in the know, the Next Big Thing.'

Rachel shook her head emphatically, unaware that she was edging towards the door. 'No,' she protested. 'Uh-uh. Not any more.'

'What do you mean? You're the toast of Paris, darling. Your face is on every street corner in the city advertising this spectacular concert. Soon, isn't it?'

'No. I mean, yes, the concert's tomorrow. But...' Rachel shook her head, struggling to maintain her grip on this conversation. 'I'm not doing it. I...left my management. The concert should have been cancelled—I'm sure it has been, in fact... They just haven't taken down the posters...'

Arabella cut through her stuttering resistance. 'I don't think so, angel. Some friends of mine have tickets. And surely you're under contractual obligation to go through with it, anyway?' Her pretty, pointed face still wore an expression of avid fascination which Rachel found sinister. She wanted to cover her ears with her hands and close her eyes to block out what Arabella was saying. *Contractual obligation?* she thought wildly. What did that mean?

'Darling, do sit down so we can talk properly.' Arabella patted the bed beside her and gave a throaty laugh. 'I'd hate to wake Sleeping Beauty over there—and, Lord, what a beauty he is. Of course that's part of the problem, isn't it? That's why you've turned your back on your fabulous but no doubt very demanding career? You've fallen in love with him, haven't you? Don't bother denying it, sweetie, because it's absolutely pointless, I'm afraid. It's written all over you.'

Rachel turned her head away. Her eyes were drawn back to Orlando's lean, elegant form on the sofa. She was suddenly too tired and too confused to think or argue any more, and she felt the denial that had sprung to her lips wither and die there.

'I'm so sorry...' she whispered hoarsely.

'Oh, darling, don't be silly!' Arabella's voice was full of concern. 'It's I who should be saying that to you. Love's never easy at the best of times, and loving Orlando Winterton... Well, let's just say you're not the first to get your fingers burned in that particular fire.' She paused, then added abruptly, 'I suppose you've slept with him?'

Looking down into her lap, Rachel nodded miserably, so missed the glint of malice in Arabella's eyes.

'Oh, dear. And that must have given you hope that your feelings were reciprocated?' Arabella reached out a hand and tucked a strand of hair behind Rachel's ear. 'Well, there's no easy way to say this, angel—but I hate to see such a lovely and talented girl throw her life away on a lost cause, so I'm going to be utterly straight with you. I want Orlando and I to give things another go. For Felix's sake.'

Rachel closed her eyes and felt her whole body tense as Arabella's words penetrated the fog of confusion in her head.

'Now, don't get me wrong,' she continued. 'I really don't believe in couples staying together just for the sake of the children—especially if one of them is in love with someone else. But the thing is, Rachel darling…I don't think that's the case here. Has Orlando *told* you that he loves you?

Rachel shook her head dumbly as hot, stinging tears gathered in her eyes and began to overspill.

'No.' Arabella held her hands up apologetically. 'Stupid question. You've hardly known each other any time, and Orlando's hardly the type to use the word freely. I think it took him a good year to finally say it to me.' She eyed Rachel thoughtfully, an expression of extreme solicitousness on her face. 'There's one thing, of course, with Orlando. One thing that's absolutely key to understanding him. He's intensely proud, as you may have guessed, and intensely private. But he will take down those barriers for people that he cares about. People he *really* cares about.'

This whole encounter had taken on a nightmarish dimension. Rachel half expected Carlos to appear in a puff of smoke, like a pantomime villain. Only the persistent throbbing in her head and the dull ache in her chest told her that this was real. That she couldn't just open her eyes and make the sound of Arabella's husky, insistent voice fade back into the shadows.

'There's something you should know about him, Rachel—something I think that, if he had any plans at all to include you in his future, he would have told you…' She paused dramatically, fixing her piercing blue eyes on Rachel, watching her intently. 'He's going blind.'

'I know.' Rachel lifted her gaze to Arabella's and for a moment saw a flash of surprise there. 'I found out by accident. I borrowed his car…there was a leaflet in the glove compartment about it and it all fell into place…'

'Ah. So he hasn't told you himself?'

'No,' Rachel whispered.

'Well, maybe he hasn't had the chance?'

Rachel thoughts flew back, for the millionth time, to last night. He could have told her then. All the time they were having dinner, or upstairs in Felix's room, he could have told her. She shook her head slowly. Arabella's hand came out and covered hers.

'Of course, it doesn't necessarily mean he doesn't love you,' she said carefully. 'It's just that it *is* a fairly major thing to keep from someone if you intend to be around them for any length of time, isn't it? It's so awful for him—we've had a *long* talk about it this evening… He says it's got worse lately. It's a degenerative condition—maybe you know that from the leaflet? It affects only the central part of the eye, which is why he can still maintain such a damned good impression of normality, but he can't see anything in the middle of his vision.' She gave a little regretful pout. 'Which means, my darling, that he's never seen your pretty face. I'm sure if he had he would have fallen in love with you on the spot.'

Sorrow and hurt were bunching up inside Rachel, making it difficult to breathe. She wanted desperately to snatch her hand away from its imprisonment in Arabella's cool grip, but felt oddly powerless. Events just kept coming at her, like a succession of waves battering an exhausted swimmer who wasn't sure she had the will to stay afloat any more.

'It wouldn't have made any difference,' she said through dry lips. 'It's you he loves, Arabella. I've known it all along.'

Arabella's mouth quirked into a smile of satisfaction as she leaned back on her bank of pillows. 'I don't know about that,' she said girlishly, twisting a lock of her streaky blonde hair round a finger. 'But, yes, in his own way I think he does. Anyway, I think we can make it work. For Felix. It's so important for him to grow up in a family environment, I think—which is why, if Orlando hadn't come back, I would have taken Felix to Brazil.'

'Brazil?' Rachel echoed faintly, her heart thudding.

'Yes. My family all live there, and he would be surrounded by cousins and aunts and uncles…which of course are no substitute for a father. '

Her blue eyes bored into Rachel's with meaningful intensity, and with a shiver of disgust Rachel recognised the veiled threat behind the words. If Orlando didn't go back to Arabella, she would take his son to the other side of the world.

Pulling her hand away, Rachel stood up. She found herself instinctively drawn back to Orlando. She couldn't help it. Right from the moment she'd first seen him she'd felt somehow that he represented home for her. Without him she felt utterly directionless.

Right on cue, Arabella spoke. 'So, what about you, darling? What will you do now? I think, in a way, all of this has worked out rather well. Your concert—your big break—is tomorrow. There's still time to go back, sweetie, isn't there?'

'But I can't. I still have Felix to look after—'

'Oh, don't be silly! You don't think I'd be cruel enough to make you stay on as nanny *now*, darling? Of course not—Orlando and I will manage. Together.'

'Oh.' Humiliatingly, Rachel felt her face crumple as sobs shook her body. 'In that case…I don't know. I can't think…'

'Well,' said Arabella firmly, 'I think you should go to the hotel now and get a good night's sleep. And then in the morning you can come back here and we'll talk about it. All right?'

Mute with misery, Rachel nodded.

Deliberately, wanting to imprint the moment on her memory for ever, she reached out a hand and touched Orlando's face. In sleep, the torment had left it, and he looked simply remote and heroic—one of King Arthur's knights, awaiting the call to greatness again. Raising her fingers to her lips, she kissed them, and gently brushed her fingertips across his exquisite mouth.

Behind her, she heard Arabella give a little hiss of disapproval. When she spoke her voice was sharp. 'Don't wake him, sweetie. There's a good girl. He's obviously exhausted, and I just want him to have a chance to rest. I think that's reasonable, don't you, darling?'

A spark of anger glowed in the darkness of Rachel's heart. Suddenly she wanted to turn round and shout at Arabella that it *was* her fault Orlando was tired, *her* fault for bringing him all this way when there wasn't even anything much wrong with her. For a dizzying moment she closed her eyes and imagined the terrible relief of standing there and unleashing all her rage and resentment and bitterness and grief onto the smug figure in the bed, but then it passed, and she was left feeling just unbearably sad.

'I won't wake him,' she said flatly. 'I just want to say goodbye. To them both.'

Crouching down beside the car seat, she dipped her head to nuzzle Felix's hair, breathing in his wonderful scent as she dropped a kiss onto his warm head. And then she stood up, looking down on Orlando while the tears streamed down her cheeks. An odd, disjointed memory of a story book she'd had as a child came back to her, where the princess's tears had fallen on the blinded eyes of her handsome prince and his sight had been magically restored. It suddenly struck her as being a horrible distortion of a happy-ever-after. She would love Orlando whether he could see or not.

'No need to make a big thing of it,' Arabella said sharply. 'You'll see him in the morning.'

It didn't make any difference. Rachel knew that this was still goodbye.

As a woman in the male-dominated world of corporate finance, Arabella de Ferrers had learned to make the most of her advantages. Her success, therefore, was due not only to her incisive business mind and excellent head for figures, but to her great cleavage, her long legs, and her instinctive understanding of how to use them.

She'd been a major player, but fate had dealt her a series of bad hands. She wasn't just fighting for a position at the top any more, she was fighting to stay in the game. And she wasn't overly troubled with a conscience when it came to sticking to the rules of fair play.

She might have lost a few of her marketable assets, she reflected thoughtfully, but she was still a formidable adversary. And she still had plenty of contacts. It had taken has a little under ten minutes to discover the name of Rachel Campion's agent and inform him where Rachel was staying.

Now all she had to do was keep Orlando here until the morning, when Rachel would be safely back in the clutches of her very grateful agent, and maintain a suitably compassionate expression when she broke the news to Orlando of Rachel's defection. Switching out the light, Arabella allowed herself an exultant smile.

That might be the hardest part of all.

There was a knock at the door.

Rachel heard it as if from a great distance. The sound meant nothing to her, so she simply ignored it. Anyway, she felt too tired, too stiff and cold, to get up and cross the room to open it.

She was sitting on a chair by the window, and had been for a long time. At the beginning—hours or days or a lifetime ago?— she had been looking out at the street below, in case a car pulled up and Orlando got out.

There had been lots of cars. Whoever would have thought that so many people would come and go in the secret hours of the night? She couldn't say at exactly what point her hopes had died. Only that as the meagre light of the new day had gradually leaked into the room it had become apparent that they were as cold and stiff as she was.

There was another knock, louder this time. Slowly she raised her head, frowning.

Maybe she'd missed him getting out of the car down on the street below? Maybe he'd come straight up to her, without stopping at the desk to ask for the key…?

With a tearing, wrenching gasp she stumbled to her feet. Her legs were shaking as hope and adrenaline surged through her, and she threw herself across the room, her arms outstretched, blindly groping for the lock on the door, wrestling with it for agonising seconds before flinging it wide open.

'*Orlando—*'

She stopped, her chest rising and falling with desperate, racking sobs as she tried to make sense of what her eyes were telling her.

There, standing in the doorway with a look of compassionate concern on his face, stood Carlos.

CHAPTER FIFTEEN

ORLANDO stormed into the reception hall of the hotel. At this hour of the morning it was already busy, with people settling bills and checking out, or waiting in little groups before setting out on whatever excursion they had planned for the day. Bypassing them all, Orlando went straight to the desk. Seeing the murderous expression on the face of this intimidatingly tall, compellingly handsome man, the couple who had been querying their bar tariff stepped aside.

'Miss Campion in the Orangerie suite?' Orlando snarled. 'Has she checked out?'

'*Pardon, monsieur*... There are other people waiting.' The small and officious concierge didn't look up from his computer screen. This was a mistake. If he had, he would have been better prepared for the moment when Orlando reached across the desk and grabbed him by the lapels of his well-tailored uniform.

'I'm sorry,' Orlando said with devastating politeness, 'but this is urgent. Just tell me...*has she checked out*?' He let go.

Throwing a look of blatant dislike in Orlando's direction, the man began tapping details into the computer. At length he looked up.

'*Non, monsieur.*'

He didn't meet Orlando's eye, looking instead at a point just over his right shoulder, where the lifts were situated. He gave a brittle smile.

'Can I have the key, please?' Orlando said harshly.

'Hold on please, sir,' the concierge said silkily. He took an eternity to come back with it, by which time the red-haired girl he had just seen emerging from the lift with her distinguished-looking companion had crossed the lobby and been ushered out into the street.

Backing away from the desk, Orlando totally missed the small, superior smile on the concierge's face. His heart was hammering a panicky tattoo against his ribs as hope churned with icy fear inside him. *She hadn't checked out. That meant she must still be upstairs. Didn't it?*

He hammered on the lift call button, and was relieved when the doors slid open straight away. But, stepping inside, he nearly blacked out with annihilating longing as he breathed in the faint scent of roses. Desperately he looked around. The lift doors were closing, shutting out the clear part of his vision, and the dark vortex at its centre obscured his view of the lobby through the narrowing gap. He opened his mouth to call Rachel's name, but the doors slid inexorably shut, leaving him shouting into the insulated silence of the lift.

Slamming his fist against the door, he felt the structure shake beneath his feet. He spun round, searching frantically for the control panel, and then gave a violent curse of rage and self-disgust as he realised he couldn't even see which number to press. Slowly, laboriously, he felt his way along them, counting.

When he finally reached the suite he threw open the door.

'Rachel!'

His voice was so raw with emotion that he hardly recognised it as his own. He strode through the horribly quiet room, knocking over a vase of flowers, flinging doors open, feeling his hopes being relentlessly slashed as each one revealed an empty room. Eventually he was back where he started, with no choice but to face the facts.

Arabella had been telling the truth for once. Rachel was gone, leaving nothing behind but a lingering scent of rose petals and his whole life in ruins.

Arabella's voice seemed to hang in the heavy, oppressively heated air. *'She's a world-class pianist with a glittering international career, Orlando. Even you couldn't be selfish enough to want her to give all that up for a life of complete isolation with a blind recluse.'*

How bloody arrogant he'd been.

He had booked this ridiculous hotel suite with such definite plans. Here, he had thought, away from the crushing familiarity of Easton, he would be able to open up to Rachel and finally hack through all the secrets and misapprehensions that lay between them like a forest of thorns. She was brave and strong and loving—if anyone would accept him as he was, flawed and damaged, she would. He'd even been hopeful enough to ask for a two bedroom suite—what he'd had in mind for her afterwards definitely wasn't suitable for Felix to witness.

But such was his own selfishness he hadn't considered Rachel herself. Her life. Had he ever really thought of her as Rachel Campion, world class pianist? Sickeningly he recalled that first night in the kitchen, her horror at his lacerated fingers, her reluctance to pick up the knife. He remembered his unconcealed disdain. Even when he'd found out about her profession he hadn't given it much thought.

What had Arabella called her? The Next Big Thing?

Rachel had tried to tell him herself, hadn't she? She had said that not playing the piano had been like losing a part of herself. And he knew exactly how that felt. Why was he surprised that she'd gone back? Arabella was right. Going after her would be nothing short of cruel.

'Querida…are you feeling better?'

Carlos looked at Rachel with infinite concern as he came into her dressing room at the concert hall. Struggling with the zip on her dress, she felt herself stiffen at his approach, and clutched the green velvet protectively against herself.

'You still look very tired. I wish you had let us take you back to the hotel for some rest before tonight.'

'I'm fine,' said Rachel coldly. 'I needed to practise.'

'You are as brilliant as ever.' Carlos's voice was like oiled silk as he trailed a hand over her rigid shoulders. 'I am so glad to have my little star back where she belongs. You have no idea how worried we have been.'

'But I left a message. I told you I was safe.'

Carlos's small eyes glittered in the harsh overhead light. 'I know, and I tried to understand that you needed some time to think. I am a fair man, *querida*. I do not blame you. Deep in my heart I knew you would come back.'

Rachel fought a tide of nausea and felt her own nails digging into her arms. How she hated herself for proving him right. How she despised her weakness for giving in and going with him. But the point at which he had appeared at the door of that stiflingly lavish hotel suite had been the lowest of her life. Her resistance, her pride, her ability to think clearly had all completely deserted her, and she'd felt so profoundly alone that she would probably have willingly gone with an axe-wielding serial killer if he'd shown her a glimmer of kindness. It hadn't even crossed her mind to ask how Carlos had found her; it had just seemed like a masterstroke of fate that he had.

'So I gathered, from the fact you didn't cancel the concert. What would you have done if I hadn't come back?'

Carlos threw back his head theatrically and waved an arm. 'I make contingency plans,' he said airily, and then quite suddenly his expression changed. 'You humiliate me enough when you leave me at the church, Rachel,' he said with quiet malevolence. 'It took a lot of money and careful PR work to contain the damage. I do not want to have to deal with that again.'

'What were you going to do?' she asked, torn between not wanting to know and needing to find out the worst.

He walked slowly around her. He was so much shorter and squatter than Orlando, she thought with a shiver of distaste. She was no longer frightened of him. Just repelled. She would work alongside him for the remainder of this tour, and then…

The thought was like plunging head-first off a cliff into darkness. Then what? Without the piano, without Orlando or Felix, *then what*?

She was so gripped by horror that she almost didn't notice Carlos's touch on her back, his fingers crawling like insects across her skin and playing idly with the zip of her dress. 'You are not the only young, slender red-headed pianist, *querida*,' he whispered, his breath hot against her neck. 'How many times do I tell you? Rachel Campion is not just a person, she is a *brand*. If you are unavailable for the concert, we get an understudy for the role of Rachel. The public do not know. The hall is big. Everyone sees red hair and they think of you.' He laughed nastily, and shivers of loathing rippled down her spine. '*That*, my little one, is the power of marketing. Brand association. Brand identity.'

Rachel stared straight ahead, transfixed. 'What about the music?' she said tonelessly. 'You might find someone who looks like me, but what about someone who plays like me?'

'Ah. Ever the artiste. Well, not all pianists have your talent, it is true. The critics, no doubt they would be disappointed. They would comment on a lack of finesse, a heaviness of interpretation…Rachel Campion does not live up to her early promise, they say, burned out so young—what a pity.'

As the implication of his words struck her there was a commotion in the corridor outside. She heard her mother's shrill voice, and then a deeper one cutting through it. The next minute the door burst open, and Rachel felt a thousand-volt surge of relief and hope as she found herself staring straight into Orlando's face.

It was blisteringly angry.

'What do you think you're doing?' said Carlos imperiously, but without stepping out from behind Rachel.

'I need to talk to Rachel.' Orlando's voice was like a rusty blade. 'Alone.'

'Impossible,' said Carlos haughtily. 'Before a performance she must not be—'

His words were choked off as Orlando reached over Rachel's shoulder and seized him by the arm, dragging him forward and twisting it up behind his back.

'You must be the bastard who forced her to sleep with you.'

Carlos made a strangled noise, which was turned into a high-pitched cry as Orlando jerked his arm further up his back.

'And then you tried to force her to marry you. You're a conductor, no?'

Carlos gave a whimper of assent. 'I imagine,' Orlando went on icily, 'that conducting with a broken shoulder wouldn't be easy. So let's just say that if you ever touch her again your career will be over.'

He thrust him towards the door. Muttering darkly and straightening his clothes, Carlos attempted to make a dignified exit.

Orlando and Rachel stood facing each other. Rachel found she was shaking uncontrollably, though he was utterly still. He was staring straight at her, his eyes dark pools of anger, rimmed by the thinnest band of pale green ice. For a long moment neither of them spoke. Then, seeming to make an effort to rein in his fury, Orlando put his hands in his pockets and came slowly towards her.

'So,' he said with quiet venom, 'you ran away again. It's getting to be quite a habit.'

She took a couple of steps backwards, stung beyond belief at the hostility in his tone. Slumping against the wall, she bent her head.

'Is that what you came here for? To tell me again that I lack courage? Because if you did you're wasting your time and your breath. I already know.'

'No.' There was an edge of darkness in his voice that sliced through her heart like a guillotine. 'I came to see if you were all right. I came to see for myself that you'd left of your own free will. That you'd made a *choice*.' He shook his head in bewilderment. 'I couldn't just let you go without trying to understand why.'

Rachel took a deep breath in, trying to steady herself, trying to steel herself against the heartbreaking necessity of lying. She was doing it for Felix. For Felix and Orlando, and their future together as father and son. It was a love worth sacrificing her own small, ravaged heart for.

'I was surplus to requirement,' she said with admirable calm. 'Felix has both his parents now. He doesn't need me.'

'What about me?' Orlando lashed out, then stopped and turned sharply away. She saw him raise his hand to his face, his long fingers massaging his forehead as he paced restlessly across the floor. Reaching the door, which Carlos had left open, Orlando kicked it viciously shut and turned back to face her. 'You don't think that I deserved some sort of an explanation? A goodbye at least?'

He leaned back against the door, looking dangerously calm and almost languorous. Only the terrifying darkness in his eyes and the tense set of his jaw betrayed his fury.

'If I'd said goodbye I was afraid you'd—say something to make me stay.'

He slammed his fist against the wall. 'Jeez, Rachel. What do you take me for? Some kind of tyrant? Is your opinion of me so very, very low that that you think I'd blackmail you to stay when you wanted to leave?'

Leaning against the wall opposite him, Rachel let her head fall back as her body was racked with anguish. Every second, with every painful beat of her heart and every deep shuddering breath, she wanted to throw herself into his arms. All her noble intentions to do what was right for Felix were suddenly engulfed by the tidal wave of need that crashed through her as she registered the strength of his emotion.

'I didn't want to leave,' she moaned. 'I didn't want to. I *had* to. For my own sanity.'

'Why?'

'Because I fell in love with you!' she shouted. 'And because you were unavailable—in every sense of the word. Sex—that was all that was on offer. The rest of you was out of bounds. I can't live like that. It'll destroy me in the end, loving someone who can't love me back. You've spent the whole time I've been with you keeping me at arm's length, and I know it's my fault for wanting too much, but I need more than that!'

His face was absolutely ashen. 'You're right,' he said through tight, bloodless lips. 'I did keep you at arm's length. But I had good reason to. I had a bloody good reason.'

'Did you?' she yelled. 'Did you really? Well, I'm glad. I'm glad all this misery isn't for nothing. But, just out of interest, maybe I could hear that very good reason now? It's far too late to make a difference, but I'd kind of like to hear it anyway.'

With a lithe movement of his shoulders Orlando levered himself from the door and stood before her, wearing a look of raw agony.

There was a sudden sharp knock on the door. 'Five minutes, *mademoiselle*!'

'*Oh, God...*' Rachel jumped, the green dress slipping from her shoulders as her hands flew to her face in panic. And then Orlando was there, holding her steady, his green eyes seeing right into the fear and insecurity inside her, calming it. 'It's OK. You're fine. Your dress...let me do it.'

Wordlessly she turned round, and the world stilled again as his fingers traced their now familiar path along her spine to the base of her dress. She let out a breath of hopeless laughter.

'What will I do without you to dress me?'

His hands closed around her shoulders and he turned her back to face him. Tilting his head back, he stared down into her face and spoke through gritted teeth.

'It's not too late.'

Rachel looked up into the face she loved for its uncompromising strength as much as for its undeniable beauty. For a moment she found herself wondering whether Felix would inherit his father's unshakable determination as well as his aristocratic features. She would never find out. But though she would never see him grow and change and become himself she still had a responsibility to make that journey as smooth as she could for him. That was why she had to do this.

'It is,' she whispered brokenly, and his grip tightened convulsively on her shoulders, as if she'd hurt him and he was tensing himself against the pain. 'I'm sorry, Orlando, but it *is* too late.'

There was another urgent knock at the door, and the voice called 'They're ready Miss Campion.'

Orlando let her go, holding his hands up as if in surrender for a second, before letting them fall helplessly to his sides. 'In that case I won't hold you back any more.'

He stood aside. Rachel was ghostly pale, trembling with the effort of holding herself together. The thought of playing in front of almost two thousand people in just a few short minutes was nothing compared with the emptiness that would come afterwards, when she came back in here and Orlando would be gone. These last few seconds seemed infinitely precious, loaded with a lifetime of meaning and feeling.

She hesitated by the door and looked at him with huge, troubled eyes.

'I just wish…' she said, in a voice that was low and filled with pain. 'I just wish you could have told me *why* you wouldn't let me near you, that's all. Because I want to know it wasn't something stupid, like the fact that you're losing your sight. You have to know that that wouldn't have made the slightest bit of difference to how I felt about you.'

Very slowly he turned his head towards her. He wore an expression of intense desolation.

'Arabella told you?'

'She did. But I found out for myself before that. At Easton.' Rachel opened the door. 'And it doesn't make you any less of a hero or any less of a father or any less of a bastard for breaking my heart. So get over it and stop hiding behind it.'

For a moment after she left he stood as if turned to stone, and then he rushed out into the corridor in her wake.

Too late. She was gone.

A few moments later a gust of air seemed to ripple through the building as it was shaken by a storm of tumultuous applause. But to Rachel, taking her place at the piano in the centre of the starkly lit platform, the applause and adulation of two thousand people was immaterial. She played for herself, and for Orlando and Felix, to express a grief that words could not adequately convey.

It was, quite simply, the performance of a lifetime.

CHAPTER SIXTEEN

London. Four months later.

'So THIS is the heir of Easton?'

Andrew Parkes leaned over his desk and peered benignly at Felix. 'Gorgeous little chap, Orlando. Very like you—and his namesake, of course. Very like Felix too.'

Orlando gave a wry smile. There was perhaps good reason for that—as Arabella had maliciously revealed in one of their final arguments, before she'd left for her new home in Dubai with her oil executive fiancé. Orlando was indifferent; all that mattered was that Felix was staying with *him*. The oil executive didn't like children, apparently.

'So…' Reluctantly, Andrew stopped blowing raspberries at Felix and cleared his throat self-consciously. At six months, Felix was distractingly sweet. 'How are you?'

Orlando shrugged. 'No change. My sight hasn't deteriorated any further. I can still get around fine. I can change the odd nappy, if I have to, though don't tell the nanny that.'

Andrew Parkes nodded. 'Excellent.' Though that didn't explain why Orlando Winterton still had the look of a man who had just been released from the torturer's cell. 'And how are you finding the…er…adjustment, mentally.'

Orlando sighed impatiently. 'I'm doing all right, Andrew. People know now. I don't hide it any more.'

Or hide behind it.

'That's a huge step forward.'

Orlando stood up, deftly holding Felix against his body with one hand, and the little boy regarded Andrew with clear Winterton eyes while Orlando stared fixedly ahead. 'It's one thing coming to terms with it for myself, but I need to know what the chances are that Felix will have inherited this too.'

Andrew looked thoughtful. 'Slim, I'd say. It's a very rare disease, and for a child to get it both parents need to be carriers of a recessive gene. We can't test for the gene yet, but obviously Felix will be very closely monitored.'

Orlando's face was dark. 'Would it make any difference if I wasn't his father but my brother was? Would that make it less likely?'

'Probably not…' Andrew replied carefully. 'I assume you ask that for a reason?'

Orlando gave a wintry smile. 'My brother was apparently devastated by my diagnosis, and Arabella very generously offered him solace,' he said sardonically. 'Naturally it's all my fault. As is Felix's death. According to Arabella, he was too upset by the prospective bleakness of my life to be able to fly safely.'

'Ah…' Frowning, Andrew rested his elbows on the desk and steepled his fingers. 'I think, Orlando, I should mention something at this point that might ease your conscience a little. I can't say too much, but Felix had also been referred to me, as you were, following a routine sight test. His appointment was the week following yours. He telephoned my secretary to cancel it. He didn't book an alternative date.'

Blood drummed in Orlando's ears as the implications of what Andrew was saying hit him. 'You're saying that maybe Felix…?'

Andrew held up a hand to stop him. 'I'm saying nothing, because that would be in direct contravention of the Hippocratic Oath. No, I am merely letting you know of your brother's change of plans. From that,' he said emphatically, 'you may draw your own conclusions, and if they lead you to the realisation that you are in no way to blame for what happened to him that's only fair. As for this little chap—Felix the second—he's no more and no less likely to inherit the condition whichever of the two of you were responsible for his arrival in the world.'

'Thank you, Andrew.'

As Orlando carried Felix carefully down the steps to the street, he thought about what Andrew had just told him. He'd discovered a lot about himself in the last four months. Mostly things that Rachel had seemed to know right from the start. Like the fact that courage wasn't only measured by medals and military honours, and heroism wasn't about wearing a uniform and dying in a far-flung place.

What Andrew Parkes had just said only served to reinforce that.

He'd been so quick to assume that Felix was the brave one, that while he had been falling apart at home his brother had been out there protecting his country, upholding the family name. But maybe, just maybe, Felix had been the cowardly one. Faced with the same challenge, Felix had opted for the easy way out. Orlando had chosen to fight.

Though at times it was a bleak and bitter struggle.

Outside, the polluted city air was warm, and the afternoon sun slanted down between the buildings onto the acid-green leaves of the trees outside Andrew's consulting rooms. Automatically Orlando's imperfect gaze sought out the place where he'd first seen Rachel's picture over a year ago, on that dark, hopeless day of his first diagnosis.

At first he thought it was his mind and his sight playing tricks on him—another instance of the brain supplying the image that it wanted to see. He blinked and rubbed a hand across his face, hardly daring to look at it again.

But it was there again. Another picture. Blurred. Only visible to him in tantalisingly small pieces. But the date on the poster was today's.

* * *

Slumped in front of her dressing room mirror, Rachel squirted the dregs from a bottle of eye-drops into eyes reddened by not enough sleep and too many tears, before making a start on repairing the ravages four months of grief had wrought on the rest of her face.

It was a warm evening in June, but she was wearing her beloved old cashmere sweater to keep at bay the chill which seemed to pervade her bones all the time these days. The tour had been a massive success; every date had been followed by rapturous reviews from critics, who claimed that she 'imbued the music with hitherto unplumbed emotional depth', and that she was a 'courageous performer'.

The latter statement was the only thing that had brought a faint smile to her lips in months. She had paid a high price for that courage. It was a legacy of her time with Orlando.

Another was that Carlos had kept a hostile but merciful distance since the night Orlando had threatened him. Her mother, who had a much less rosy opinion of Carlos since he had tried to replace Rachel with a stand-in, was now much more of an ally, and while Rachel would never forgive Elizabeth for all the years when discipline had replaced love, at least she understood better now. Love was so very, very sore.

Glancing up at the clock, Rachel steeled herself for the knock at the door. Tonight was the last date of the tour, and though she was tired, she was also dreading life beyond the final encore. She was afraid that without this nightly exorcism, the demons inside her would slowly smother her.

The door opened and Elizabeth put her head round it. 'All set, darling?' she enquired brightly. Rachel nodded. 'Take off that dreadful old sweater, then, sweetie, and I'll see you afterwards.' Blowing a kiss, she disappeared.

Reluctantly Rachel got to her feet and peeled the sweater over her head, then stood for a moment looking at her reflection in the mirror. She was wearing another dress in her signature dark ivy-green, made of satin this time. Its neckline plunged down to a narrow band of beading beneath the bust, from where the fabric fell with bias-cut fluidity, artfully skimming the new roundness of her belly.

The other lasting reminder of her time with Orlando.

It was a glorious evening.

The sky, which had been an unbroken dome of Wedgwood blue all day, was now dotted with feathery fine tufts of cloud, stained blush-pink by the setting sun so they looked like the marabou trim on a bride's negligée. After two weeks of torrential rain the unexpected arrival of summer had created an expansive mood amongst the concert crowd on the balcony of the Bankside Hall. They lingered over their cocktails and champagne until the last possible moment, before making their way unhurriedly inside for what promised to be a fine programme of music.

Following the rave reviews, tickets to the concert had sold out with lightning speed, but tonight there were a few unclaimed seats as, swayed by the sudden spell of good weather, people had taken off to the country or to Ascot. Therefore it hadn't been difficult for Orlando to arrange a last-minute seat at the back of the hall.

What had been more problematic was persuading the girl on the door to let him take Felix in.

In the end she had been powerless to resist the old magic formula of devastatingly good-looking man with small baby and, muttering anxiously about losing her job, had let him slip through the doors when the lights were dimmed. She'd been rewarded with a kiss on the cheek, which more than made up for the worry of being found out.

With Felix fast asleep in his arms, Orlando slumped into his seat and steeled himself, as an eruption of applause told him that Rachel had just walked onto the platform. Tipping his head back against the seat, he could just make out her vivid hair, shining beneath the bright spotlights like flame.

For a second there was silence as the audience settled, and

then the opening bars of a Debussy prelude floated through the warm evening air.

An audible breath of collective contentment rose from the audience. Until that moment Orlando hadn't given a thought to the music, but as the sound filled the rafters and ran in rippling currents over his tautly stretched nerves he was transfixed. It reminded him so poignantly of when Rachel had been at Easton, and all the nights he'd sat at his desk, wrestling with life and death issues on the other side of the world, and she'd reached out to him through the cold blackness and reminded him of his own humanity. The irony was so perfect: he'd been handling a defence crisis, and all the time his own defences had been being stealthily undermined. And he hadn't even realised until it was too late.

Far too late.

Could there be any words more poignant than those?

Time ceased to exist as he sat there, hovering in a state of blissful painlessness, suspended between having her and not having her. He had grown so used to waking up alone, as yet another dazzling dream of Rachel faded, leaving him with his monochrome and lonely reality, that just breathing the same air as her for a couple of hours was, he realised desolately, better than being without her altogether. And, after so many months of firmly steering his thoughts away from Rachel, it was the greatest relief to just give in.

At length he was aware of the piece coming to an end, and for a moment there was absolute silence in the cavernous hall as everyone sat, still spellbound. Then there was an explosion of clapping.

In his arms Felix gave a start, raising his head and whimpering slightly before settling again. Orlando held his breath. Then below, on the rostrum, Carlos cued the orchestra into a Scarlatti sonata, and Felix, roused a second time, gave a loud, indignant wail.

Carlos made a vicious slashing motion with his baton and

whirled imperiously around. Instantly the orchestra ground to a ragged halt.

'A *baby*?' said Carlos in outrage. 'What is the meaning of this?'

Orlando got abruptly to his feet. Felix was crying in earnest now, the sound drifting up into the roofspace, thin and plaintive. In the audience curious muttering broke out as heads turned and feet shuffled, and then there was a collective gasp as the pianist herself got up and peered out into the crowd.

The murmuring was hushed again as everyone held their breath and waited for her reaction. Straining forward in their comfortable cherry-red seats, they eagerly anticipated a display of diva rage to complement the glowering indignation on Carlos Vincente's face. But instead they saw a look of naked hope and longing as Rachel Campion shielded her eyes against the bright lights that were directed on her, straining past them to look into the darkness beyond.

'Felix?'

It was no more than a whisper, but the microphone above the piano picked it up and amplified it so that above the crying of the baby everyone heard the low note of yearning in her voice.

'Orlando?'

As if operated by a central remote control, every head turned to the back of the hall. The man who stood in the central aisle, holding a crying baby in his arms, was tall, romantically dark and breathtakingly handsome. He also looked as if he had been struck by lightning.

The atmosphere in the hall was suddenly charged with electrifying tension. No one moved, and the only sound was the heart-wrenching cries of the baby.

Rachel sat down at the piano again. Softly, and with infinite tenderness, she began to play.

Chopin's *Nocturne in E Minor* rippled from her fingers in a magical, shimmering rainbow of sound, every note vibrating with love and longing. Even though the conductor had now left the rostrum, one by one the members of the orchestra joined in, until the hall was filled with the purest sound.

It was as if angels hovered in the rafters.

In the spotlights Rachel's tears glistened like falling diamonds. Her face was that of a suffering Madonna—full of pain and adoration and tortured bliss.

The Bankside Hall held one thousand three hundred people. By the time the music melted back into a shivering silence Felix was amongst the few who weren't crying. For a moment there was an absolute absence of sound. And then the muffled thud of a door shutting at the back of the hall.

When everyone turned to look, the man with the baby had gone.

And when they turned back so had the pianist.

The network of passages behind the stage at the Bankside was labyrinthine. Rachel's breath came in desperate gulps as she hurtled along them, alternating between hope and terror as she desperately tried to find her way to him.

He was probably here with Arabella, her head very firmly said. Or else she'd gone somewhere else for the evening and left him at a loose end with Felix…

But he had come, and that was something, her heart cried wildly. He had come, and she couldn't let him leave without asking to see him again. She knew how much he loved Felix—he had a right to know about his other child. Her baby.

The sound of her heels on the tiled floor echoed madly in the stark corridors as she ran, so she paused to slip them off and carried on, not caring what she looked like to the few straggling musicians and backstage staff she passed. Rounding a corner, she found herself on the mezzanine balcony that rose up from the Bankside's famous Art Deco entrance hall.

She rushed to the railing and looked down.

With the concert still technically not ended, the place was deserted—except for one man crossing the austere white space towards the door. There was no mistaking those massive shoulders, the narrow hips and long legs, the slow, deliberate walk. Or the infant, now quiet, in the car seat.

'Orlando... *Please*... Wait!'

His hand was on the door.

'You can't just leave like that!' she said wildly, the pain in her voice echoing around the stark walls.

As if in slow motion she watched his arm fall back to his side. Seeming to tense himself, as if in anticipation of some terrible blow, he turned round. His expression was rigidly controlled, his narrow eyes dark and hollow.

'I have to.'

She gazed down at him. Her chest was heaving with the exertion of running, and also with painful locked-in emotions. The air seemed to have been squeezed from her lungs and replaced with razorblades, and her eyes searched his face for answers to the questions she hardly dared to ask.

'Arabella? Is she waiting for you?'

For a second he looked almost bewildered, shaking his head as he said irritably, 'Arabella? She's gone. We were never together.'

Rachel could feel the metal railing biting into her aching fingers. 'But Felix...' she said desperately. 'She said if you weren't together she would take Felix...'

Bitter understanding suddenly flooded Orlando's face. With deliberate care he set Felix down on the floor at his feet. 'Another of Arabella's sophisticated tactics,' he said acidly.

A tiny spark of tentative hope glowed somewhere in the darkness of Rachel's barred and shuttered heart. 'Why are you here?' she asked, trying to keep the pleading note out of her voice. 'Why did you come?'

Below her, Orlando was standing perfectly still, perfectly straight, his face an emotionless mask.

'To see you.' He gave a sudden ironic laugh. 'To hear you. Whatever. It was worth it. You were astonishing.'

'But you're a philistine,' she protested, unable to stop the hope that was now spreading like wildfire through her whole body. Holding onto the balcony railing for support, she started to move along it towards the stairs, never taking her eyes off his pale, tense face. 'You said so yourself…. You don't even like music. You burn pianos.'

He gave a deep, shuddering sigh. 'You wouldn't believe how much I've changed.'

She had reached the stairs now, and she began to run down them on bare, silent feet towards him. Tears were streaming down her face as she came to a standstill in front of him on the second step from the bottom. Adrenaline and love and the same gut-wrenching desire she had always felt whenever she looked into his ocean-coloured eyes fizzed through her, making her brave.

'I don't want you to change…' she whispered fiercely. 'I love you just the way you are.'

Very slowly he lifted his hand and held it out towards her. The smile he gave her was one of unbearable sadness as he tilted his head back slightly, as if preparing himself for the firing squad.

'Oh, Rachel…' he said resignedly, 'I love you too. Far, far too much to ruin your life. You're too bright, too beautiful, too talented to throw yourself away on me. This is where you belong—and if I had any doubts about that before, tonight has put them all to rest once and for all. If we were to…' He faltered, and an expression of fathomless suffering flickered across his face. 'I'd only stand in your way, and I can't do that. I won't.'

For a moment Rachel couldn't speak, couldn't take in what he was saying. The words were like silvery, shimmering snow-flakes, and for a second all she could do was watch them in wonder, terrified that if she tried to catch them they'd melt away. Hesitantly, she brought her hand up to his, and with infinite tend-erness her fingertips brushed his outstretched palm.

'Again…' she breathed, her face streaked with tears. 'Say that again.'

Their fingers tightened, twisting together, locking fast, so that they were holding onto each other as if from either side of a deep and unbridgeable ravine.

'I love you,' he said harshly. 'I love you, but I won't hold you back. I won't take you away from everything you've worked for. You were right. Your hands are far too brilliant, far too precious for everyday life at Easton. I can't do it to you.'

'You don't have to.' Joy sang out of her voice, falling onto his bowed head like sunlight breaking through cloud. 'I'm doing it to myself. As of tonight, I'm retiring.'

'*No—*'

'Yes,' she said tenderly, emphatically, lifting her chin and gazing at him in a blaze of defiance and love. '*Yes*. This time, Orlando Winterton, you have *no choice*. As of tonight I'm starting my maternity leave, and there's nothing at all you can do about it.'

His head whipped violently upwards. His face was ashen, but his eyes burned with terrifying emotion.

'*What?*'

Gently she pulled the hand that was still entwined with hers downwards, and placed it on the slippery satin over her small bump.

'See?' she whispered.

And then suddenly he was pulling her into his arms, bringing his mouth crashing down on hers, and they were devouring each other with all the desperate longing of the past four months, all the hope of the next lifetime. When he finally pulled away Orlando couldn't tell whether the wetness on his cheeks was from her tears or his own.

As his hands moved wonderingly over her rounded stomach, moved upwards over the cold, slippery satin to the new fullness of her breasts, her eyes never left his face. The fierce, dazed longing there told her everything she needed to know.

'There's an expression…' she said slowly. 'An old proverb that says "Love is blind, but marriage restores its sight"…'

Orlando took her face in both his hands, gazing down at her with his intense, mesmerising stare. 'I don't want to have my sight restored,' he said gravely. 'I don't need to, because when I'm with you I see things more clearly than I ever did before. God,

Rachel, I do want to marry you. I want that more than anything.' He paused, frowning. 'But can you really live with this illness?'

She smiled into the clear pools of his eyes. 'I can't live without it. Because it's part of you, and I can't live without you. Your life is my life. Your problems, your joys, your triumphs, your children…all mine. Because you see things in me that I didn't know were there. You give me courage.'

He laughed, though his dark lashes were wet with tears. 'You're going to need it if this baby's a boy. Believe me, Winterton brothers are a nightmare.' Still holding her face between his hands, he pressed a kiss to her quivering lips, feeling them part beneath his, welcoming him into the darkness of their private heaven. He felt drunk with longing, drunk with love.

Behind them there was an embarrassed cough. 'Miss Campion… Excuse me…'

'Mmm?' Rachel murmured against Orlando's mouth.

'The audience are wondering if there will be an encore… They want more.'

Orlando groaned. 'They're not the only ones,' he said with a rueful grin, taking a step backwards and giving her a little push in the direction of the hall. 'Go.'

'I don't have to…'

'You do. Over a thousand people are waiting for you.'

'You and Felix are the only ones who matter.'

'We'll wait as long as it takes.'

She was halfway across the hall, but then she ran back to him and stood on tiptoe to brush her mouth across his ear, her fingers lightly caressing his neck as she breathed very softly, 'Five minutes. And then I'm yours—exclusively, for ever.'

Closing his eyes, he smiled languidly into her fragrant hair as her touch and the whisper of her breath against his ear sent shockwaves of ecstasy through his entire body.

Five minutes suddenly seemed a hell of a long time…

EPILOGUE

THE rose-petal-pink sun drifted gently down behind the garden's old brick walls and violet shadows gathered, darkening to deepest indigo beneath the sheltering limes. Felix ran ahead, the sound of his clear, pure laughter floating through the honeyed evening air as he reached the fountain which bubbled up through the stones at the secret heart of the garden.

Rachel's design for the old rose garden had been faithful to the original in spirit rather than in actual detail. Old-fashioned blooms still spilled abundantly over arches and pathways, but these had been re-laid to her exact specifications, using specially chosen materials. In the gentle days of the previous autumn, as her bulk had swelled, she had paced and sketched and directed a team of gardeners who had been under strictest instructions from Orlando not to let her do anything remotely strenuous. The completion of the garden had coincided with the arrival of a delicately beautiful baby girl, whom it had seemed only right should be called Rose.

Pausing now, in the golden summer twilight, a cool, moisture-beaded bottle of champagne clasped in one hand, Rachel looked back. The garden was at its most intoxicatingly perfect—ripe with blossom, heavy with perfume—but her joy in the achievement was nothing compared to the familiar surge of deep-down, wrenching love she felt as she watched Orlando walk towards her with his sexy, long-limbed stride, their daughter in his arms.

Although she was the first Winterton girl for three generations, seven-month-old Rose had the dark hair and thrill-seeking energy of all her male forebears, and she kicked and wriggled delightedly in her daddy's easy grasp.

The neck of Orlando's white wedding shirt was open, his tie long since discarded. A couple of hours ago, in a private ceremony in Easton's church, he had reverently added a plain band of old gold to the finger of Rachel's left hand that already bore the Winterton rubies. Afterwards, coming out of the church into the drowsy late-summer afternoon, the new Lady Ashbroke had taken her bouquet of apricot roses, gathered that morning from the garden, and laid them at the feet of Felix's angel.

They had returned to Easton, where all the estate employees and Rachel's new friends from the mother-and-baby group in the village had mingled happily on the lawn and drunk champagne beneath a soft, forget-me-not blue sky. It had been perfect. And yet Orlando had found himself longing for this moment, when he could have Rachel to himself again.

Beneath his bare feet the slate pathway felt like warm silk as he followed the ribbon of smooth stones set into it. This began at the doorway at the end of the lime walk and got gradually wider as the path wound its way to the centre of the garden, meaning he could instantly orientate himself. Rachel's idea, and just one of the many millions of ways she made his life better.

She made *him* better.

He followed her to where the stone seat stood, in its arbour of frothing white roses, and stooped to set his daughter down on the circle of flat cobbles around it. Instantly Rose hitched herself up onto her plump pink knees and, cooing with satisfaction, scuttled off in her precocious crab-like crawl to find her beloved Felix and the water. Orlando sat down beside Rachel, taking the glass of champagne she put into his hand. Her wedding dress was a simple knee-length shift of palest coffee-coloured silk, and he dropped a kiss onto her bare creamy shoulder.

'Are you sorry we're not jetting off somewhere exotic for a

honeymoon?' he murmured. Her skin was like the velvet of sun-warmed peaches.

'No.' She smiled, bending her head to expose the curving sweep of her rose-scented neck to his lips and sighing with pleasure. 'I'm glad. I love it here too much. At home.'

The shadows stretched and deepened, and the first tiny diamond stars flickered in the lilac sky above them. The children's laughter and muted shrieks of joy rose like soft moths in the hazy, fragrant evening. Sipping champagne, Rachel let her head fall back as Orlando's beautiful fingers moved languidly down her arm, trailing rapture. Through half-closed eyes she gazed at him, feeling the familiar unfurling hunger inside, watching as his mouth spread into a slow smile of recognition.

'Lady Ashbroke, would I be right in thinking that you're giving me *that* look?'

She breathed a low, wicked laugh and slipped her hand between the buttons of his shirt, feeling the muscles of his taut stomach tighten beneath her palm. 'How did you guess?'

'I can *feel* it.'

'How does it feel?' she whispered huskily.

'Exquisite.' He drained his glass of champagne and stood up, pulling her to her feet. 'But, unless you do something about it soon, extremely uncomfortable. Come on—time for bed.'

Rachel quirked an eyebrow. 'Us or the children?'

'Both.'

Laughing, Rachel gathered up a protesting Rose, raining kisses down onto her face and her fat little hands, while Orlando lifted Felix high, setting him on his shoulders. Together they made their way back up the path to the house through the blue evening haze.

A vast disc of gold hung over the rooftops of Easton as they approached.

'Moon,' said Felix sleepily, pointing. 'Big yellow moon.'

'Honeymoon,' said Rachel quietly, as Orlando's fingers closed around hers, his thumb caressing her palm. 'A perfect honeymoon.'

And, in every way possible, it was.

HARLEQUIN *Presents*

EXTRA

HIRED: FOR THE BOSS'S PLEASURE

She's gone from personal assistant to mistress—but now he's demanding she become the boss's bride!

Read all our fabulous stories this month:

MISTRESS: HIRED FOR THE BILLIONAIRE'S PLEASURE
by INDIA GREY

THE BILLIONAIRE BOSS'S INNOCENT BRIDE
by LINDSAY ARMSTRONG

HER RUTHLESS ITALIAN BOSS
by CHRISTINA HOLLIS

MEDITERRANEAN BOSS, CONVENIENT MISTRESS
by KATHRYN ROSS

HARLEQUIN *Presents*

HARLEQUIN *Presents*

*Introducing an exciting debut
from Harlequin Presents!*

Indulge yourself with this intense story
of passion, blackmail and seduction.

VALENTI'S
ONE-MONTH MISTRESS
by Sabrina Philips

Faye fell for the sensual Dante Valenti—but he
took her virginity and left her heartbroken. She
swore *never again!* But he wants her back,
and what Dante wants, Dante takes....

Book #2808

Available March 2009

Look out for more titles from Sabrina Philips
coming soon to Harlequin Presents!

REQUEST YOUR FREE BOOKS!

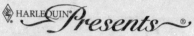

2 FREE NOVELS
PLUS 2
FREE GIFTS!

YES! Please send me 2 FREE Harlequin Presents® novels and my 2 FREE gifts (gifts are worth about $10). After receiving them, if I don't wish to receive any more books, I can return the shipping statement marked "cancel". If I don't cancel, I will receive 6 brand-new novels every month and be billed just $4.05 per book in the U.S. or $4.74 per book in Canada, plus 25¢ shipping and handling per book and applicable taxes, if any*. That's a savings of close to 15% off the cover price! I understand that accepting the 2 free books and gifts places me under no obligation to buy anything. I can always return a shipment and cancel at any time. Even if I never buy another book, the two free books and gifts are mine to keep forever.

106 HDN ERRW   306 HDN ERRL

Name	(PLEASE PRINT)	
Address		Apt. #
City	State/Prov.	Zip/Postal Code

Signature (if under 18, a parent or guardian must sign)

Mail to the **Harlequin Reader Service:**
IN U.S.A.: P.O. Box 1867, Buffalo, NY 14240-1867
IN CANADA: P.O. Box 609, Fort Erie, Ontario L2A 5X3

Not valid to current subscribers of Harlequin Presents books.

Want to try two free books from another line?
Call 1-800-873-8635 or visit www.morefreebooks.com.

* Terms and prices subject to change without notice. N.Y. residents add applicable sales tax. Canadian residents will be charged applicable provincial taxes and GST. Offer not valid in Quebec. This offer is limited to one order per household. All orders subject to approval. Credit or debit balances in a customer's account(s) may be offset by any other outstanding balance owed by or to the customer. Please allow 4 to 6 weeks for delivery. Offer available while quantities last.

Your Privacy: Harlequin Books is committed to protecting your privacy. Our Privacy Policy is available online at www.eHarlequin.com or upon request from the Reader Service. From time to time we make our lists of customers available to reputable third parties who may have a product or service of interest to you. If you would prefer we not share your name and address, please check here. ☐

HP08R

The Inside Romance newsletter has a NEW look for the new year!

Same great content, brand-new look!